PAYBACK

Also by
roy glenn

Is It A Crime   MOB   Drug Related

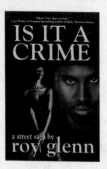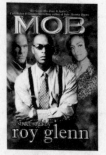

Anthology:

Girls From Da Hood

Gigolo's
get lonely too

PAYBACK

a street saga by
roy glenn

PAYBACK

Urban Books
74 Andrews Avenue
Wheatley Heights, NY 11798

ISBN 0-7394-6375-6

Printed in the United States of America

This is a work of fiction. Any references or similarities
to actual events, real people, living, or dead, or to real
locals are intended to give the novel a sense of reality.
Any similarity in other names, characters, places, and
incidents is entirely coincidental.

Dedicated to you

Chapter One

Shy tried to stay as calm as she could with a gun pointed at her head. She'd just been taken hostage from Black's Paradise, a reggae club on the beach in Freeport on Grand Bahama Island. She glanced over at her abductor and then to his stomach. He was losing a lot of blood. "This man is gonna die unless you do something to stop the bleeding," Shy yelled at the driver.

"How bad is it, Julio?" the driver asked.

"It's bad, Sal," Julio said as he continued to hold his gun to Shy's head.

"Hold on, man. I'll get you to a doctor."

The sight of Julio's blood took Shy back a couple of years to the night she got shot. She thought she was going to die sitting alone in the back seat of that car.

Shy could hear the cop yelling, "Freeze!" as she turned and pointed her gun at him. The bullet hit her in the upper right chest, near her shoulder. Shy shot back as she fell, and hit the cop with one shot to the head. When she got up, she decided not to take the time to ponder the ramifications of killing a cop, picked up the briefcase and proceeded down the fire escape. That night changed her life forever, Shy was thinking as she felt Julio's gun in her side.

"What's your name, sweetie?" Sal asked.

"Cassandra Black," Shy answered defiantly.

"Cassandra Black, as in Mike Black is your husband, Cassandra Black?"

"Yes." Shy said, hoping that his name carried some weight, but unsure whether it was a good or bad thing. *Where are you, baby?* Shy thought. Mike Black had always been there for her. When somebody was trying to kill her, it was Black who provided her with the lead that she needed. And it was Black who intervened when Hector told her no money, no product. In the time that she'd known Mike Black, he had saved her life three times, if you count him sending Bobby and Freeze to save her when she had gotten in over her head. *I need you to save me now.*

"Shit," Sal said quietly. "So, that club was Black's club? What the fuck am I askin'? Black's fuckin' Paradise. Shit!" He pulled out his cell phone and dialed a number.

It was answered on the first ring. "Que pasa?"

"This is Sal. I need to talk to Papi."

"He is very busy right now. Why don't you call him back in about an hour?"

"I need to talk to him now! Just give him the fuckin' phone."

"Okay, Sal, hold on. Papi!" He continued in Spanish, "Sal dice necesito hablar con él ahora," letting Papi know that Sal needed to talk to him now.

Papi took a deep breath and reached for the phone. He set it down on his lap, lit a cigar, and took a sip of his tequila before picking up the phone. "Sal, what is so important that you must talk now? You should

learn to relax, take things easy. You think with your mind. You move with your body. Mind and body are inter-related, and you must learn to maintain control of your own body. Relaxation techniques can help you to think clearer, focus more, and concentrate."

Now it was Sal who took a deep breath. He could hear what sounded like a woman laughing in the background. "I'm sorry to bother you, Papi, but shit went bad for us in the Bahamas."

"Really? What happened?" Papi said calmly.

"Julio went wild and just started shooting up the place."

"I did not go wild, Papi!" Julio screamed in his defense. "Those men were DEA!" Julio yelled as Shy held her breath. The last thing she wanted was for Julio to get excited and shoot her accidentally.

"Now he's sayin' that the money guy was DEA," Sal told Papi.

"So, you didn't get the money?"

"No, Papi, we didn't get the money."

"Why not, Sal?"

"The money guy wasn't alone. After Julio shot the money guy, this other guy opened up on us and we had to shoot our way outta there. Then Mike Black's wife starts shootin' at us with a pump. She killed Manuel. Did you know that it was Mike Black's club we was meetin' in?"

"You ask too many questions, Sal."

"All I'm sayin' is that we had to take her hostage to get outta there."

Papi laughed out loud, thinking that things were working out better than he planned. "I want you to take her to Miami and call me when you get there."

PAYBACK

"I know this guy from New York. He's a crazy muthafucka."

"I know who he is, and that is exactly why I want you to take her to Miami."

"I don't think you understand. Mike Black is connected to some very powerful people. I don't think we want to fuck with him. I think we should drop her off somewhere and be done with her."

"Sal," Papi said, no longer laughing. "I like you, Sal, and we have not worked together for very long, so I'm going to tell you something, and I know that I'm only going to have to tell you this one time. I don't pay you to think. When you work for me, I demand your respect and your loyalty. I expect you to believe in me, and to do exactly what I say without question. Is that understood, Sal?"

"Yes, Papi," Sal said and rolled his eyes.

"That is good. Now, take her to the boat. The captain will take you to Miami, and you will call me when you get there. Comprendé?"

"I understand, Papi," Sal replied reluctantly and drove toward the dock.

Papi hung up the phone and turned to his associate. "I'm sorry, my dear," Papi said.

"What was that about?" she asked.

Papi looked her and thought for a second. "This may be of particular interest to you. Sal had to take a hostage." Papi paused for effect. "Her name is Cassandra Black."

"Give her to me," the woman said and smiled.

"Why, so you can kill her?" Papi laughed.

"Yes."

a story by roy glenn

While Sal drove, trying to heal his broken ego, and Julio grimaced in pain, Shy thought about her situation. She tried to convince herself that she wasn't scared, not really anyway. She was raised around all types of the criminal element: gangsters, hustlers, and dealers. These guys were no different. She could and would kill them if she got the chance. Shy had to laugh at herself as she thought back to the days when all she was good at was pulling her gun and talking big shit. Shy had shot at people not knowing if she hit anyone. But things were different now. She had stood in front of a man, looked him in the eyes, pulled the trigger and watched him die.

Shy was relieved that whoever this Papi character was, he wanted her alive; at least for the time being. And the only reason for that was because she was married to Mike Black. He controlled a profitable gambling, prostitution and number running business, and although they lived in the Bahamas now, his name was still influential in the States. Once again, he had saved her life.

Mike loved Shy deeply and wanted to insure that nothing would ever happen that would put her life in jeopardy. That was why he had moved Shy out of New York to the Bahamas. Black thought that she would be safe in their quiet island paradise.

She felt a chill as the idea that she might never see her husband again washed over her. She loved him so much and hated the fact that they had fought the night before. *If Michael had been there, none of this would be happening.* Shy didn't want their fight to be the last thing they shared.

PAYBACK

"Black's not here because we had a fight last night," Shy remembered telling Nick. He came to the island to see Black, who he hadn't seen in years, and to meet Shy. "He left the house and I haven't seen him since. He may be in New York or he may be right here on this island. I don't know."

"What was the fight about?" Nick asked.

"You hit it dead center when you said I was bored. I miss New York and I want to go home. I really haven't made any real friends down here." Shy leaned forward and whispered, "Probably because I can't understand what they're sayin' half the time." She laughed. "And these women . . . Oh God, why they all gotta fall all over my man? And it's not just these island bitches. The tourists are worst. Why do they have to have their half-naked asses all up in his face, gigglin' over every word he says, while I'm standin' right there? I mean, Nick, I try to rise above that 'cause I know he really ain't like that anymore, but it's hard. Bitches ain't got no respect."

"Sometimes gettin' bitches' respect is overrated. As long as Black shows you respect, fuck them bitches. You're his wife."

"I know that, Nick. And Michael shows me nothing but love and respect. And I love him so much for that. I know that's just something I got to get past. I guess I'm just a jealous woman, and I'm tired of it, you know what I'm sayin'?"

Maybe Nick was right. As long her man showed her love and respect, she couldn't be stressed over it. It was all about trusting him, and since she believed in her heart that he would never do anything to put their relationship in jeopardy, what was the point? Shy would take it all back now if she could, because that

6

wasn't her real issue. The real issue was her legal status. Shy was wanted for murder, but her lawyer, Wanda Moore, was able to get the murder and conspiracy to commit murder warrants dropped. Without the murder weapon or any witnesses to place Shy at the scene, they had no murder case.

Wanda Moore always wanted to be a lawyer and she was good at it. Wanda had gotten Mike and his associates out of more cases than she could remember. She was smart, careful, and just a bit ruthless. In addition to being their lawyer, Wanda managed the money, making a small fortune for her partners, in addition to developing a reputation as an excellent entertainment lawyer. However, despite Wanda's efforts, there was still a warrant out for Shy for conspiracy to distribute that to this point she hadn't made any headway with.

"The fight was really about me wantin' to go back to New York," Shy told Nick.

"But you can't, because of the conspiracy charge," Nick said.

"Michael lost it when I told him that I would rather go home and do my time than stay down here. I don't want to be on the run for the rest of my life, Nick. I want to be free."

Sal pulled up at the dock and he looked back at Shy. "Now listen, we're gonna get out of this car and go to the boat. You're gonna go quietly. Some people seem to think that you've got some value, so you get to stay alive for a little while. But if you try to get away or call for help, I'll put a bullet in your brain. You understand?"

PAYBACK

"I understand," Shy said.

Sal got out of the car and pulled Shy out. He moved down the walkway quickly, practically dragging Shy along as he headed for the boat. Julio held his stomach and followed behind them as best he could.

As they made their way to the boat, Shy looked around the crowded dock and hoped that she saw someone she knew. You know, somebody who would question why this man was dragging her along, and do something to help or at least get word to Mike.

That's when she saw him. Shy didn't know what his name was, but she recognized him from the club. *He's practically a regular.* Shy had seen him many times laughing and talking with Mike and Jamaica. But the only problem was he wasn't looking in her direction.

Knowing that she would have to do something to get his attention, Shy pretended to stumble and fall. "Ouch!" Shy screamed, acting as if she was in pain and grabbing her ankle. That got his attention, as well as a few other people.

"All right, sweet cheeks, get up," Sal said as Julio caught up.

"I can't! I hurt my leg."

"I said get up," Sal demanded, grabbing Shy by the arm and pulling her to her feet.

"Where are you taking me?" Shy asked as she struggled just enough to put on a good show, but not enough to get herself killed.

"We're taking a little trip to Miami. Now, stop fuckin' around and get on that boat," he commanded and pointed at the boat. They continued walking. Shy looked straight at the man and mouthed the words, *Help me.*

Chapter Two

Nick hung up the phone and lay across the king-sized bed at the Lucayan Beach Hotel. He looked out the sliding glass door at the Caribbean Sea and tried to clear his head. He got up, walked over to the mini-bar, and got out a bottle of Johnnie Walker Black. Nick felt bad, very bad about allowing Shy to be kidnapped. *What else could I have done? What could I have done to save her?* There was only one answer. He could never have been there in the first place.

And what would he say to Black?

How would Nick explain to him that he was not only the reason the shooting started, but that he had a shot, but was too slow taking it?

He went to the door and looked out. Nick finished the small bottle of Johnnie Black and gave some thought to the fact that he had hung out in New York the night before, caught an early flight, and had been up the better part of the day. He did close his eyes

9

during the flight to the Bahamas, but now, he suddenly felt tired.

Nick lay across the bed and his head began to spin. He realized the he and Shy drank quite a bit that afternoon. He closed his eyes and began to think back over what had just happened.

"Excuse me a minute, Shy. I'll be right back." Nick got up and walked over to a man he thought he knew, sitting alone at a table by the door.

"Roman, Roman Patterson?" Nick asked.

The man didn't answer at first. He looked at the door and then slowly at Nick. "Nick Simmons?" he said quietly and looked back at the door. "What are you doin' here?"

"I'm visiting some old friends." Nick started to sit down.

"Get away from me, Nick. I'm waiting for somebody," he said practically in a whisper.

"What?"

"I'm DEA, Nick. Get away from me."

Nick turned quickly and walked away, just as Sal, Julio and Manuel entered the club and sat down at the table with Roman. Nick went back to the bar and sat down. Shy came over to him.

"What was up with that? You didn't know him?" she asked.

"He's DEA." Nick saw the expression on Shy's face. "Calm down. He's not here for you."

Nick and Shy looked on as the four men talked and laughed like old friends, until Julio glanced in Nick's direction. Julio stood up and looked directly at Nick, took out his gun and shot the DEA agent in the head, then turned and fired on Nick. Customers at Black's club began running out the back door, turning over tables in their wake, while others dove on the floor.

"Get down!" Nick yelled at Shy.

Shy ducked down behind the bar while Nick fired wildly and took cover behind a table. Sal and Manuel broke out semi-automatic weapons and began firing at him. They had Nick pinned down as they moved toward the door.

Shy reached for the pump. "Finally a little excitement on this rock." She rose up, took aim, and fired at and dropped Manuel. Shy took cover as Sal and Julio began shooting at her. This time it was Nick that came up blasting. He hit Julio, and Julio went down.

Shy stayed low as she moved toward the end of the bar. She stood up and fired the pump just as Sal ran out the door. Nick came out from behind the table as Shy moved toward the door. With her back turned, she didn't see Julio get up.

"Shy! Behind you!" Nick yelled and aimed his weapon, but it was too late. Julio had grabbed Shy and pointed his gun to her head.

"Drop it!" Julio yelled. Shy threw away the pump. "You too, drop it!" he yelled at Nick.

"Let her go!" Nick said, taking a step closer.

Julio fired, barely missing Shy. "I'll kill her!"

Nick knew he could shoot Julio in the head before he got a shot off, but before he was able to, Sal burst through the door, firing that semi. It gave them enough time to get out the door with Shy. By the time Nick got outside, they were gone.

As he drifted off sleep, he acknowledged the fact that his intoxication definitely played a role Shy's kidnapping. With his level of skill, Nick should have been able to drop all three of the bandits, semi or not. He shot Julio, but Julio was still able to get up and walk out with Shy. If he had taken the shot, would he have hit the target or Shy? Nick tossed and turned and the nightmare began again.

"Bobby put the gun down!" Mike yelled.

"I'll kill you!" Bobby screamed at Nick.

Mike put his gun to Bobby's head. "Bobby please," he said quietly. "Take the gun out of his mouth and put it down."

"Don't think this is over. I'll kill you!" Bobby shouted. "And that bitch!"

Nick sat straight up on the bed and reached for his gun. He was sweating and breathing hard. Slowly, he began to calm down. He looked over at the bed next to him; there was a man lying down. Nick aimed his weapon at the man. With the barrel of the gun, Nick poked the man in the back. "Get up. Nice and slow," Nick said as he backed away and the man began to move.

"Don't you think I unloaded your gun before I laid down?"

"Black," Nick said as Mike Black sat up on the bed.

"Hello, Nick. Damn, it's good to see you." Mike stood up and held out his arms. Although he was glad to see him, Mike would have preferred that it be under better circumstances than this. Mike was pretty excited when Wanda called and said that Nick was on his way to the island to see him. Now this had to happen.

"Good to see you too, Black." The two men embraced. "How long have you been here?"

"Not long. You still havin' that same nightmare?"

"Yeah." Nick nodded his head. Mike understood; memories of that night haunted him too. His two closest friends at each others' throats. "Why didn't you wake me up?" Nick asked.

"I tried to wake you up, but you were dead to the world. I heard you and Cassandra had a lot to drink."

There was an uncomfortable silence that drifted between them. "So, you know what happened?"

"Yes," Mike said and sat down on the bed. "I talked to Wanda after you called her. She told me what happened. I went by the club and talked to the cook."

"I'm sorry, Black," Nick said as he sat down and started to tell his story.

"Never mind that now. Get up and let's go. You can tell your story on the way."

Nick stood up and got two other guns out of the suitcase. "Where we goin'?"

"Eight Mile Rock."

While Mike drove, Nick told Mike exactly what happen that afternoon at Black's Paradise. Mike listened without comment until they reached a house off the main road. "Let's go," Mike said as he got out of the car. Nick followed Mike to the door. He knocked twice and the door opened. A man with an AK47 stepped to the side to let them in.

"He here?" Mike asked.

"In the back," the man answered and escorted them out the back door to the pool. There were four men, all armed, sitting around the pool. Three of them jumped to their feet when they saw Mike. Slowly, the fourth man turned around. He smiled when he saw Mike coming toward him.

PAYBACK

"What's up, Black?" Jamaica stood up. Then he saw Nick. "Is that Nick?"

"That's him, Trouble Man in person," Mike said.

"What's up, Jamaica?" Nick said, remembering that Trouble Man was what they used to call him when they were growing up. At the time, it was because of Nick's fondness for the Marvin Gaye song. Now, at this time, the name took on a whole new meaning.

"Been a long time, Nick," Jamaica said, reclaiming his seat. "You still drinking that Johnnie Black?"

"Yeah, but I'll pass. I think I've done enough drinking today," Nick replied and sat down.

Mike walked over to the bar and poured himself a glass of Remy Martin. "You heard anything yet, Jay?"

"The word on the rock is they come to do business. They go 'round talkin' 'bout they gon' make big money. Them say that Conchie Joe have plenty money."

"Nick, when they left, did they have the money with them?" Mike asked. "Where was the dope?"

"I didn't see any drugs or money change hands. And now that I think about it, I didn't see Roman with anything that might have had money in it."

"Maybe they were just meeting to set up the buy," Nick said.

"Maybe," Jamaica said. "But me hear that the deal was to be done today."

"But if the deal was to get done today, then where was his backup? You can't sit there and tell me that the DEA is about to do what sounds like a major bust, and the agent is in there by himself. And even if today wasn't the day, why didn't he have any backup? It just doesn't make sense." Mike walked over to the pool and sat down on the diving board. "You got names on these bandits?"

"Not yet, but me have me brethren out lookin' for them," Jamaica said. "Me have someone at the airport and at the dock. Them have to charter a plane or a boat to get off the island."

"Send someone around to all the people we know that charter. If they try to get off the island, I wanna know about it," Mike said as the phone rang.

Jamaica answered. "Hello."

"Me find a man at the dock," one of Jamaica's men said. "Him say that he see Shy and two men get on a boat. Him think he hear them say they goin' to Miami."

"Him sure 'bout that?" Jamaica asked.

"Me don't know. I just tell you what him tell me."

"What was the name of the boat?"

"Destiny."

Chapter Three

Jamaica wasted no time giving Mike the information he had just received. Mike picked up the phone
and made arrangements to have a chartered plane
meet them at the airport. Then he called Bobby in New
York. "What's goin' on down there, Mike? You find
her?" Bobby asked.

"No. I need you to meet me in Miami."

"You got it. I'll call you from the airport."

"Let me talk to Freeze," Mike said.

"He had to go handle something. I'll tell you about
it when I see you."

"Okay, you get down here as soon as you can. Let
me speak to Wanda."

Bobby handed the Wanda the phone and left the
office at Cuisine. "Hello, Mike," she said. "Have you
heard anything yet?"

"Yeah. Do you have anybody in Miami?"

"We got a couple of good people. What do you
need?"

"I need you to find out everything you can about a
boat named Destiny. I wanna know where it's docked

and who owns it, and find out fast. I'm on my way there now."

"You find Nick?"

"He's with me."

"He was with Freeze last night. He can tell you what Freeze is dealing with."

"You just find out what's up with that boat, Wanda," Mike said and hung up the phone. "Jamaica, you have the brethren meet me at the airport with whoever gave them this information. I wanna talk to him myself." Mike turned to Nick. "What's goin' on with Freeze?"

"Huh?" Nick answered, not knowing what Mike was talking about.

"Bobby said Freeze had to go handle something, and Wanda told me that you were with him last night and that you could tell me what Freeze had to go handle."

"There were some guys posted up, tryin' to roll at Doc's place last night. Freeze thinks they work for Derrick Washington, calls himself D-train. He used to be Chilly's lieutenant."

"Curl? That bitch nigga ain't got the heart to take Freeze on," Mike said, thinking that somebody must be backing D-Train up.

Jamaica sat in the front seat and talked on his cell phone while one of his men drove. Nick sat quietly behind the driver while Mike stared out the window. Naturally, his mind was on Shy, hoping that she was at least unharmed, if not safe. But there was something, a few things, actually, about this that were bothering him. First off, why would somebody plan a drug deal in his place? Anybody who was anybody who was connected to the game knew who he was and knew that Black's Paradise was his place, and the one thing Mike Black didn't tolerate was drug dealing. Then he couldn't get past the DEA agent being in there with no backup.

Mike looked over at Nick and he leaned toward him. "I'm sorry, Black. This is all my fault. I was too slow taking the shot."

"Don't worry about it. What's done is done. Besides, I should have been there. Something I wanna ask you, Nick. This DEA agent, what was his name?"

"Roman Patterson."

"This guy, this Roman Patterson, how well did you know him?"

"I knew him pretty well. We were in the same unit for two years when I was in the Army."

"What kind of guy was he?" Mike asked. "Was he a team player or a cowboy?"

"Team player, no doubt. Always about procedure, everything by the book."

"See, Nick, that's what's bothering me. Cowboys go in alone, without any backup, 'cause a cowboy always thinks that he can shoot or fight his way out of anything. Like you, Nick."

"Me?"

"Yes, you." Mike laughed. "I heard you rolled up in Rocky's place by yourself," he said, noting that Nick had rolled up in a den of drug dealers and killers by himself.

"Twice."

"Risky business."

"I seem to remember you fallin' up in a bunch of places by yourself. So, if I am a cowboy, I learned that shit from you," Nick said.

"I only did that shit when I knew I would be all right. If I thought there was a possibility that shit would get wild, either you or Freeze or Bobby was coming with me."

"You knew that we had your back," Nick said, now proud of the life that he ran away from for years.

"That's what I can't get past. What was your boy doin' up in there without backup?"

"We'll find her, Black," Nick said, trying to sound reassuring.

"I hope so, Nick. I hope so," Mike said and looked out the window. "It's still good to see you, Nick."

"It's good to see you too, Black." *Good to be home,* Nick thought.

While Mike stared out the window, he recalled the argument he had with Shy the night before. Thinking back on it now, it wasn't worth it. He knew that all that shit Shy was talkin' about him and other women was just a smoke screen to mask what was really bothering her. But if he really wanted to be honest with himself, Shy did have a point. If he wanted to, he could do something to discourage women from literally throwing themselves at him. In his mind, he wasn't doing anything, so there wasn't a problem. But apparently, Shy had a different perception of what was going on, and after all, perception is reality.

Shy felt like women openly showing their affection for her husband was disrespectful. But to Mike, it was all business, making sure his customers, especially the women, were having a good time. Happy women come back, stay longer, and make men spend more money. Strictly business. Nothing more. Mike loved Shy, and nothing any of those women had to offer was of any interest to him. He knew that, and believed that Shy should know it too. Mike felt like Shy should trust him.

Even though that wasn't her real issue, Shy raised it so strongly that Mike let it get under his skin. So, when Shy finally got around to what was really bothering her, he was on fire from what he considered her repeated attacks on his fidelity and commitment to their relationship. The truth of the matter was that Shy hadn't really been all that happy on the island.

"It's not you, Michael, or anything that you're doing. Please believe that. I just wanna go home," Shy said to him the night before. "And if that means that I have to go to jail, then I would rather do that than spend the rest of my life here." That's when he lost of mind. But he knew now that he shouldn't have. If going back to New York would make her happy, and she believed it so strongly that she was willing to do time, then he should have been willing to hear her out. *How bad could it be?* With his money and contacts, he could have easily had the case heard before a sympathetic judge, and Wanda could have pled it down to something minor.

But the truth of the matter was that Mike wanted Shy out of New York. He believed strongly that her life was in jeopardy every second that she was there, not only because of what she was doing, but also because of him. His enemies knew that she would be his weakness, and Shy would be a way for them to get to him, and he wasn't havin' it. It was safer for her if both of them were out of the city and out of the game. Or so he thought.

When they arrived at the charter plane, Jamaica's men were waiting with the man who saw Shy being abducted. Mike recognized him as soon as he saw him. His name was Harold Elgin. Mike had known Mr. Elgin during the days when he was a number runner back in New York, before circumstances forced him to return home to Freeport. The moment Mr. Elgin saw Mike coming, he rose to his feet. "Mr. Black," he said as Mike shook his hand.

"Thank you for taking the time to talk to me," Mike said.

"No problem, but your friends here didn't leave me with any choice." Mr. Elgin turned to Jamaica. "You should teach your men some manners, you know. Respect for their elders would help, maybe."

Mike stepped in front of Jamaica's men. "You will show this man respect. The same respect you show me."

"Yah mon, respect, no," they echoed as Mike turned his attention to Mr. Elgin.

"Please accept my apology for their disrespect, Mr. Elgin," Mike said as the two walked away together. "These young boys don't have any respect for anything except power and money."

"Not like the old days, you know. Back then, you show a mon respect until he proved himself unworthy of that respect. But under the given circumstances, I understand."

"Tell me what you saw."

"I was down by the docks earlier today when I heard some commotion. When I look, I see your wife on the ground. Two men were standing above her. She didn't appear to be hurt. As I think back, I believe that she was trying to get my attention."

"What makes you think that?"

PAYBACK

"Because when I turn to see, she was looking at me the entire time. As they drag her to she feet, she continue to look at me. And I am sure she mouth the words *help me*. When I move closer, I hear her ask 'where are you taking me?' The white man say they were taking a little trip to Miami."

"Are you sure about that?"

"I may be an old mon and not worthy of young mon's respect, but I can still hear."

"Did you recognize the men?"

"No. I never see them before."

"What they look like, Mr. Elgin?"

"I didn't get a really good look, but as I say, one was white and the other was of Latin descent. It appeared that he was hurt. I say this because him move slow and hold his stomach the whole time."

"Anything else you can tell me about them?"

"No, that is all I can tell you. Mr. Black, I am sorry to say that I did nothing to help your wife. It happen so quickly, and I don't carry a gun anymore."

"No need to apologize, Mr. Elgin. If you had tried to help her, those men would have killed you," Mike said as Nick walked up on them.

"The plane is ready, Black. We gotta go," Nick said.

"Thank you, Mr. Elgin. You've been a big help getting this information to us," Mike said as he walked toward the plane.

"No problem, Mr. Black."

Chapter Four

Freeze walked into Cynt's, a gambling club they had run for years. He had received a call from Cynt that there were some men who had posted up in the back of her spot, and they appeared to be selling drugs. The night before, he and Nick had a run-in with two other men who were trying to set up shop at another one of the spots they ran. Freeze was confident that these were not the same men, because those men were no longer breathing.

As he wandered around the spot looking for Cynt, Freeze was surprised but not shocked to see Travis Burns sitting by the bar, enjoying the company of two dancers. Travis, along with Jackie Washington and Ronnie Grier, were a robbing crew that made Freeze plenty of money. This was the first time that he had seen Travis since Freeze killed Ronnie over a business matter concerning his long-time female associate, Pauleen. After that, Travis and Jackie did an occasional job, but only if there was enough money involved and absolutely no risk.

23

PAYBACK

As Freeze walked toward Travis, he looked around for Jackie, who, unlike Travis, was gambling at Cynt's all the time. Not too long after Ronnie's murder, Jackie approached Freeze about her desire to have someone assassinated, but when she told him that the person was Me'shelle Lawrence, Travis's ex-girlfriend, Freeze declined and told Jackie to get over it. However, every time Jackie looked at Travis and saw the pain in his eyes, she knew that she wouldn't *get over it* until Me'shelle was dead.

"Mind if I join you?" Freeze said as Travis turned slowly and looked at him.

"This is your world, Freeze. I'm just trying to live in it."

"I hadn't seen you around much lately, Travis. What's been up?"

"Nothing, man. Just trying make a living, same as always," Travis replied. He had a feeling that it was Freeze who killed Ronnie, or at the very least, had him killed, but he had no desire to die trying to get revenge.

"I'm just sayin', you don't come up here anymore like you used to, and you have Jackie bring me my taste from your jobs."

"Yeah, well, Jackie's up here all the time doin' her thing anyway. Why not let her do it?"

"Yeah, okay, whatever." Freeze looked around the room. "Jackie here?"

"Of course she is. She's downstairs doin' her thing. Why?"

"You strapped?"

"No."

"I may need you and her to back me up," Freeze told Travis, even though he knew he could handle the

24

situation without him. It was more important to know where his head was. "And I need to know if I can count on you."

"You know you can," Travis said. "Like you said, whatever went down was business, not personal, and got nothing to do with you and me," Travis said to let Freeze know that he knew what was going on, but he was still loyal to him.

"Here," Freeze said and discreetly passed a Travis a gun.

"I'll go get Jackie," Travis said.

Freeze followed Travis downstairs to the gambling area where, as expected, they found Jackie, doin' her thing. Only nowadays, Jackie wasn't losing at poker anymore.

Early one morning, around four A.M., Mike Black came into the gambling area while Jackie was literally losing her shirt. She waved and smiled when she saw him standing directly across from her, and Mike nodded his head in response. Jackie thought Mike Black was sexy from the first time she met him. Although she'd never admit it anyone, Jackie had the kind of crush that a young girl has on her teacher. It had gotten to the point where Jackie thought about making herself available for him.

Mr. Black, Mike Black, but you are so married. So, we can be cool or whatever, but I gotta respect your wife, Jackie told her mirror one day.

Mike stood and watched while Jackie continued drop to money on losing hands. Once he had seen enough, Mike went and sat down. When Jackie lost all her money and got up from the table, Mike motioned for her to join him.

PAYBACK

"Bad night," Mike said to her, stating the obvious.

"No more than any other night." Jackie laughed, trying to make light of it.

"Freeze says that you're good people; that you and your boy are good earners. But you're here a lot. Drop a lot of money." Mike signaled a waitress for a drink.

"I'd say that was the truth."

"It's the way you play," Mike said nonchalantly.

"What do you mean?"

"I watched you play. I could tell when you had a good hand, and when your cards weren't shit. I could tell when you were nervous. I could even tell every time you had a strong card, and when you were bluffing."

"Could you let me in on it, or is it a secret? I lost a lot of money to the house too. Your house."

"No, I don't mind tellin' you, Jackie. It's written all over your face. It's your eyes, actually."

Jackie smiled. "So, you were looking at my eyes?"

"You have very pretty eyes, but they betray you every hand. All anyone your gambling with has to do is watch your eyes."

"Anything else?" Jackie asked as the waitress set a glass of Remy Martin VSOP in front of Mike and asked her if she wanted anything.

"Hennessy."

"You're reckless and greedy."

"Reckless and greedy!" Jackie barked, looking very incensed. "What do you mean by that?"

Mike took a sip of his Remy. "Before I answer your question, let me ask you one."

"Okay, go ahead," Jackie said excitedly. This was the longest conversation she'd had with Mike, and she planned on dragging it out for as long as could. *And that voice, hmm. Maybe I gave up on you a bit too soon, Mr. Black, Mike Black.*

"Are you trying to make money gambling, or is this just a sport to you?"

"I'm trying to make money, no doubt. But I would be interested in hearing you explain the difference between the two." *I'd be interested in hearing you explain how grass grows.* "If you have time. I know that you're a busy man, and I appreciate you taking the time to talk to me." *I can't believe you said that.*

Mike looked at Jackie and let out a little laugh. "If you're gambling for sport, you really don't care if you make money or not. You just enjoy the game, the tension, the anticipation, and the camaraderie; that's sport. But when you gambling to make money, then that's all it's about—money; fuck all the rest of that shit."

"From what you see, which one am I?"

"You gamble for the sport of it. That's what makes you reckless and greedy." Mike paused and then went on to explain his point. "When you got money sittin' in front of you, you make reckless bets, and when you lose, you try to laugh it off, like it's only money."

Jackie had to laugh because she knew it was true. "That's me."

"You chase the big pots." Mike paused to emphasize his point. "Greedy. And you chase them with weak hands, and since we already talked about your inability to bluff, that makes you reckless and greedy."

"Damn," Jackie said slowly. "You really have been watching me."

PAYBACK

"Watching you lose, Jackie. Watching you lose money to me," Mike said and sat back in his chair.

"You have any advice for me? 'Cause I really am trying to make money. Yes, I enjoy the game, the tension, the anticipation, the camaraderie, all that good shit, but I need to make money. I ain't making money like I used to."

"Then you have to learn some discipline. Get yourself and your emotions under control like you would be when you're doin' a job. And the most important thing is that you know how much money you want to make every time you sit down. When you're gambling, you're gonna win some and you're gonna lose some. But if you're any type of player, at some point during the night, you are going to have in front of you the amount of money you wanna make. Get up and say goodnight."

"Discipline."

"Jackie, I've seen you with ten, fifteen grand in front of you and then watched you lose it all. Discipline. You see, what the house wants is to keep you there and keep you coming back, because sooner or later, you're gonna lose."

With that thought in mind, Jackie made a few changes the next time she sat down at the table; changes not only to her look, but to her attitude. *Focus and discipline, baby, 'cause Jackie is here to get paid.* She figured that if they were paying that much attention to her face, she would give them something else to look at. Her new "uniform" became a tight red leather jumpsuit that zipped up the front, which she opened just far enough to give everybody an excellent view of her cleavage. She even wore a push-up bra to make the twins outstanding.

a story by roy glenn

On this particular night, her attire was black leather jacket and pants. Jackie had on sunglasses, and her hair hung over the frames. When Travis and Freeze approached her, Jackie was raking in a nice-sized pot. Travis tapped her on the shoulder. "Jackie."

"What's up, Travis?"

"Let me holla at you, Jackie."

Jackie turned around and looked at Travis and saw Freeze standing next to him. "Hello, Freeze." Jackie pulled back from the table and stood up. "This must be something important."

"Of course it is," Freeze said and looked around the table. "Otherwise I wouldn't bother you." This stopped any grumbles about Jackie leaving before they got started.

Jackie looked down at the money she had in front of her, trying to decide whether she needed to come back. "Fellas, as much as I'd love to stay here and continue to take your money, I gotta say goodnight."

Once they were away from the table, Jackie asked, "What's up?"

"I need you to watch my back," Freeze replied. "You armed?"

Jackie unbuttoned her jacket and opened both sides to reveal her now signature push-up bra and a 9-millimeter in each holster. "Always armed and extremely dangerous."

Travis and Jackie followed behind Freeze until he saw Cynt coming toward him. "Where they at, Cynt?" Freeze asked.

Cynt looked around her spot. "There were three of them, but I don't see them now," she replied. "No, wait. There they are."

PAYBACK

"Where?"

Cynt pointed them out. "The two of them over by the bar," she said, and Freeze wasted no time heading in their direction.

Travis and Jackie had to walk quickly to keep up with Freeze. As he walked, Freeze took a gun out of his left pocket and held it close to his side. Travis and Jackie took out their guns and Freeze grabbed a bottle off a table as he passed.

"Hey, muthafucka!" Freeze yelled over the music.

One of the men turned toward him. At that moment, Freeze smashed the bottle into his face and pointed the barrel of his gun in the face of the other. "Thought you dumb niggas woulda learned something from last night. Maybe this will convince y'all," Freeze said as he cocked the hammer.

As Freeze prepared to shoot, he didn't see the third man, who Cynt had told him about, pulling out his gun. But Jackie did.

"Freeze! Look out!" Jackie yelled. She raised her weapon and fired twice, hitting him in the chest with both shots.

Freeze fired his weapon and killed one of the men. Travis pointed his gun to the head of the man Freeze busted with the bottle.

"No!" Freeze yelled. "Don't kill him."

With his gun still pointed at the man's head, Travis took a step back slowly. Freeze grabbed the man's shirt with one hand and a bottle with the other. "You tell D-Train to stay the fuck out my spots!" Freeze yelled and smashed another bottle into his face before dragging him out into the street. "Take those two to the parlor."

a story by roy glenn

Travis looked at Jackie, who was still standing there with her gun raised. Travis took the gun out of her hand and put his arm around her as they left the spot. "Don't worry, Jackie. You did what you had to do."

Chapter Five

It was after 11 P.M. when Mike and Nick arrived at the airport in Miami. As soon as they got off the plane, Mike turned on his cell phone and it rang.

"I'm at the airport. Where are you?" Bobby asked.

"We just got here. We're going to rent a car. Meet us there."

While Mike talked to Bobby, Nick stood by and listened nervously. This would be the first time that he saw Bobby since the night Bobby threatened to kill him. After that night, Nick joined the Army.

He became part of a special operations unit. On their last assignment, they were stationed in South America, working on an illegal drug eradication effort. They were killing drug dealers, blowing up drug plants, and seizing financial records. However, something went wrong on their final assignment, and the plant blew up with most of the unit still inside. Only three members of the unit, Nick, Jett Bronson, and Monika Wynn got out alive.

They were flown back to Fort Bragg, where they were promptly debriefed and processed out. A man who called himself Uncle Felix approached them the day after. He recruited them to do jobs for him that required their special skills. Jett's specialty was electronic surveillance, and computers. Monika's specialty was munitions. Nick's specialty was weapons and special tactics.

Felix set them up in a front business as private investigators. To maintain their cover, they actually did some surveillance jobs. The real money was in doing those little jobs for Felix; hacking into computer systems, some light demolition, and the occasional termination. They would do jobs that couldn't be done through normal channels.

It was after Chilly's wife, Gee, hired them for a missing persons case that things started to go wrong. When it was all over, Felix and their Army commander, were dead, as was Jett. Monika was in the hospital after an attempt on her life. Nick had flown to the Bahamas to recuperate after the ordeal, and that was when all hell broke loose in Black's club.

And now he was standing here with Mike, knowing he had no choice but to face Bobby again after all these years. Even though he didn't think that Bobby would pull out his gun and shoot him on sight, the idea of finally having to confront Bobby made Nick very apprehensive.

Before all the shooting started, he had talked openly about the situation with Shy, more openly than he had with anybody. Shy told him that it was about betrayal. When Nick betrayed Bobby's trust, she pointed out, "You said you felt like you betrayed everybody."

"And?" Nick asked.

"That includes you. You betrayed yourself. And that's what hurts you," Shy told Nick. "So, now that you know the whole story, you're gonna have to forgive yourself for what happened. You were just a pawn in whatever game this woman was playing. Maybe when you forgive yourself, it will be easier for you to ask Bobby to forgive you." Nick understood that, and he even pretty much agreed with her.

But that was then. Now Shy had been kidnapped, and Bobby was in Miami to help Mike look for her. Nick would have preferred better circumstances to put this Camille business to rest.

Thoughts of that night when Bobby wanted to kill him had haunted Nick for years, like a bad dream that never ended. Bobby, with his gun in Nick's mouth, screaming that he would kill both Nick and Camille. It should have never happened, but Nick had never met any woman like Camille. It was the way she looked at him when they made love. For years, when he closed his eyes, it was Camille's eyes looking up at him.

It began the first time Nick saw Camille and she walked right up to him. She put her left hand on his chest and looked into his eyes. From that moment on, Camille had Nick and she knew it. Each time he saw her after that, Camille made that point clear. When she called, Nick would come. What Camille wanted, he got for her. What she said, Nick did, without so much as a kiss. He felt like a fool carrying this around all these years. It was time for him and Bobby to make peace and finally lay their beef over Camille to rest. *After all, the bitch has been dead for ten fuckin' years.*

When Nick and Mike arrived at the rental car counter, Bobby was already there and had begun the process of renting a car. Mike walked up behind Bobby and tapped him on the shoulder.

"I hope you got a black car."

Bobby turned around quickly. "No, it's red," Bobby replied as he shook Black's hand. Then he looked at Nick. Bobby nodded his head to acknowledge Nick's presence before returning his attention to the reservation clerk. Nick stood back awkwardly and watched as Mike leaned on the counter and whispered to Bobby, who would glance over at him and the two of them would laugh. Nick felt like an outsider.

Once the rental was secured, Mike and Bobby came toward Nick. Mike passed by, but Bobby walked straight up to him.

Nick started, "Look, Bobby, I just wanna say—"

Bobby cut him off. "You can save whatever it is you think you gotta say to me. That shit is over, been over since the day somebody put two bullets in her brain." Bobby started to walk away, but turned around quickly. "Damn, it's good to see you, Nick."

"You ladies coming?" Mike asked.

"Yeah, we're coming," Bobby said as he hugged Nick.

Once they were in the car, Mike called Wanda. She told him where he could find the boat Destiny docked. He asked if she was able to find out who the boat was registered to. She informed him that it was registered to somebody named Esperanza Velasquez, and gave Mike her address. "You heard from Freeze?"

PAYBACK

"Yes, but I'll explain that to you when I see you," Wanda replied.

When they arrived at the place where Destiny was docked, Nick took a look around the area and could see one man standing guard on deck with an AK. "I can pick him off from here," Nick told Mike and Bobby.

"Bullshit," Bobby said quietly, not wanting to attract any attention.

"Go ahead," Mike said with a laugh as Nick put a silencer on his gun and took aim with his .45. He fired one shot and the hit the guard in the head.

Mike turned to Nick with a very serious look. "Why couldn't you save Cassandra?"

"She pours a mean drink."

"She sure does," Mike said quietly, dropped his head a little and started for the boat. Even though he was doing his best not to show it, this shit was fuckin' with Mike, and it was fuckin' with him bad. No matter how he felt about it, he had to remain calm and strong. But it wasn't easy. He couldn't blame Nick for what happened. The only one he could blame was himself. He should have been there.

If I hadn't lost my mind when Cassandra said that she would rather go to jail, then I would have been there to save her, instead of being off somewhere pouting like some spoiled fuckin' child.

The worst part of it was that he felt so helpless. Well, at least now he was doing something. Mike wanted to scream, to hit somebody, to hurt somebody, to cause somebody pain. Mike wanted to kill somebody. He made a vow then to kill everybody involved, no matter how long it took.

When they got on the deck, Nick checked the pulse of the man he'd shot. "He's dead," he said and began to drag the man below.

"You sure this time? I mean, he ain't gonna get up and kidnap me later, is he?" Bobby asked.

"Stop fuckin' with him, Bobby. He probably feels bad enough already," Mike said.

"Oh, it's all right when you fuck with him, huh?" Bobby asked as they went below.

When Bobby opened the door with his gun drawn, he found two men. Julio was lying on the bed with his eyes closed, and another man was seated in the chair next to him. As soon as he saw Bobby come through the door with his gun pointed at him, the man stood up and raised his hands.

"Please don't kill me."

Nick patted down the man to be sure that he wasn't armed, then took a look around the room and left to check the rest of the boat. Mike stepped up to the man.

"Who are you?"

"My name is Carlton, Daniel Carlton. I'm a doctor. I was brought here by force to treat this man."

"You can put your hands down," Mike said and put his arm around the doctor. "Is he gonna be okay?"

"He suffered a gunshot wound to the abdomen. He is very weak from the blood loss. I think that he'll be fine if he is allowed to rest and give the wound time to heal," the doctor went on to explain.

"Where's the woman they had with them?"

"I don't know. I left her and the other man on deck, and I came down here to treat this man."

"You know what this other man's name was?"

PAYBACK

"No, I don't. Nobody said any names, and they always spoke in Spanish, except when he was talking to me."

"Was he a white man?"

"Yes."

"The woman, was she all right?" Mike asked.

"Yes, from what I could tell. But she looked scared."

"Did you hear them say where they were goin'?"

"If they said where they were going, they said it in Spanish, and I wouldn't have understood them anyway. Sorry I can't be any more help," the doctor said. It was obvious from the way his voice cracked when he talked that he was scared too.

Nick came back into the room. "Rest of the ship is clean."

Mike picked up the doctor's bag, handed it to him. "You can go now, doctor. I think that we can handle it from here." Mike reached into his pocket and pulled out some money. He peeled off five hundred-dollar bills and handed them to the doctor, then he turned to Nick. "Would you mind showing the doctor out?"

"Not at all."

"Thank you, thank you," the doctor said as he left the room, thankful to be leaving with his life.

When Nick returned, Bobby slapped the shit of out Julio. "Wake up, asshole! Where's the woman you took from the club?" he demanded to know. Julio opened his eyes and looked at Bobby and then to Black. When he saw Nick, his eyes opened wide.

"Remember me?" Nick asked.

"He feels that pain in his gut, Nick," Bobby said and punched Julio in the face. "Yeah, he remembers it was you that put that bullet in him," he said and punched Julio in the face.

Mike put his foot on Julio's stomach and put his weight on it. "Who are you working for?"

Julio screamed in pain and spit at Black. "Usted no puede entender una palabra yo digo y yo no le diría nada si usted puede," Julio said in Spanish.

Nick stepped up and leaned over Julio. "Puedo . . . y usted hace," Nick replied in Spanish.

"What did he say?" Bobby asked.

Nick turned to Bobby. "He said we can't understand a word he's saying, and that he wouldn't tell us anything even if we could. I told him that I can understand him, and he will tell us."

"I didn't know you spoke Spanish, Nick," Mike said, grinding his foot into Julio's stomach. Julio winced in pain.

"Yeah, I speak Spanish, French, Italian, Japanese, several Arab dialects and a little German," Nick said.

Bobby started laughing. "Damn, I remember when you could barely read."

"Yeah, well, things change," Nick told Bobby.

"Ask him who he's working for, Nick," Mike said, trying to stay on task.

"Quién es usted trabajando para?"

"El me matará si yo le digo!"

"Qué le hace piensa que haré si usted hace no?"

"What y'all sayin'?" Bobby asked.

"I told him I'll kill him if he doesn't tell me."

"Oh, that's good, Nick. Really original," Bobby said with a laugh.

"This is taking too fuckin' long," Mike said. "Nick, hold his arm." Nick grabbed Julio's arm and Mike shot

39

him in the hand. Julio screamed and cursed in Spanish.

"Where the fuck is my wife?" Mike shouted.

"Dónde está la mujer que usted raptó?" Nick demanded.

"Yo no sé!" Julio screamed.

Mike shot him again, this time in the kneecap. "Where the fuck is she?" Mike yelled.

"Don't you see these boys ain't playing with you?" Bobby said to Julio. "I know you understand what I'm saying to you, and I know you understand this," he said and shot Julio in his other kneecap. Once again, Julio screamed and did some more cursing in Spanish.

"Dónde está la mujer que usted raptó?" Nick asked him again.

"Yo no sé donde, pero Sal la tomaron a Nueva York."

"He says he doesn't know where, but Sal took her to New York."

Mike took his foot off Julio's stomach and started to walk away. "Bobby."

"Say goodnight, Gracie." Bobby raised his gun and shot Julio twice in the head.

Mike turned to Nick, "So, Mister I-speak-Spanish-French-Italian-Japanese-several-Arab-dialects-and-a-little-German, can you pilot this ship?"

Both Nick and Bobby laughed. "Carver 404, twin Mercruiser engine; cruising speed, seventeen knots; max speed, twenty-five knots. Yeah, Black, I can pilot the ship."

"Good. Take us out to sea so we can dump these bodies," Mike said. "We'll take care of things down here."

While Nick went on deck to take the ship out to sea, Mike and Bobby cleaned the room of blood and wiped down any area that might have their fingerprints, just in case the doctor decided to report what he had been involved in that night to the police.

Once they were finished cleaning, Bobby came up on deck and sat down next to Nick. "I'm gonna learn how to sail one of these things so next time I can be up here chillin', enjoying the night air, and you can be the cleaner."

Nick laughed. "It ain't that hard, Bobby. You want me to show you?"

"Nah, not tonight," Bobby replied as he yawned and stretched. "You know we ain't sleepin' no time soon, right?"

Nick nodded his head slowly then turned to Bobby. Despite what Bobby said about the shit being over, there was something Nick felt he had to get off his chest.

"Look, Bobby, I'm sorry."

"For what? 'Cause I can't sail this ship?" Bobby joked.

"No, about Camille."

"Listen, Nick, I can't be mad at you for fuckin' her when she set the pussy out for you. She was a ho, and I shouldn't have gotten so strung out on her. I mean, shit, the bitch fucked Freeze and Mike then she fucked me, throw the pussy at you from the first time she saw you, and she wanted to fuck Wanda. And those are just the ones we know about."

"I didn't know that until I read that journal she was keeping," Nick said and laughed. "You're right. She was a ho."

41

PAYBACK

"It's me who could be sayin' sorry to you. I should have never pulled my gun on you. I've regretted that shit every day since. I should have never let a woman, any woman, come between us. You're like my brother, Nick, so let's just put that shit behind us. Cool?" Bobby stood up and extended his hand.

"Cool," Nick said and accepted his hand.

Mike came up on deck and joined Bobby and Nick. "How far out are we?"

"About ten miles," Nick responded.

"That's far enough. Come on, Bobby." Mike and Bobby carried the bodies up on deck. They weighted the bodies down with whatever they could find and tossed them overboard. Once they were done, Nick turned the ship around and headed back to the dock.

Chapter Six

Bobby got behind the wheel and started the car. They went to check out the address of the woman who owned the boat, but the house was in darkness.

"Where to now, Mike? Back to the airport?" Bobby asked.

"Not yet."

"Where you wanna go then?"

"Let's go see Hector. He hangs at a club called La Covacha. It's on Twenty-fifth Street."

"Hector?" Nick questioned. "Hector Villanueva?"

Mike nodded.

"I remember that guy," Nick said.

Back in the day, Hector Villanueva used to buy from André Hammond, who controlled most of the drug traffic in the area. Mike worked for André as enforcer, collector and at times, his personal bodyguard. Even though he did business with them, André hated Puerto Ricans, so he was killin' Hector on price. Mike did Hector a favor and introduced him to Angelo Collette. Angelo and Mike were in the same

43

PAYBACK

homeroom class in high school. Back in the day when they were both freelancing, they did a few jobs together. They robbed a few jewelry stores, took down a payroll or two. Now Angelo was a very important man. After Mike introduced Hector to him, Hector started buying his product from Angelo at a better price than André had been giving him.

Mike was forced to call in the favor when Shy had business with Hector and he was being tough on the negotiations. Mike was able to get Hector to do business with Shy. At that point, Hector considered their business together concluded, but he and Mike had something else more personal in common.

"You think Hector has something to do with this mess?" Bobby asked and glanced over at Nick.

"Not really," Mike replied casually. "But you never know."

"Yeah, right." Bobby laughed. "You just wanna fuck with Hector, see if you can go up in Nina while we're down here, don't you, Mike?"

"I remember Nina," Nick said. "That was one beautiful woman. Seeing her would be enough reason for me to go fuck with Hector."

"No, I just wanna ask him some questions."

As Bobby drove off, Nick thought about the years he had missed. He glanced in the back seat at Mike and then over at Bobby. He was glad to be able to close the door on that part of his life, after all these years, to finally say that he was sorry to Bobby. Maybe now he could take Shy's advice and forgive himself for betraying Bobby and fucking Camille. *Even if she was a ho who was fuckin' everybody.*

It was 2:30 in the morning when Bobby pulled up in front of La Covacha, one of the most popular spots for Latin music in Miami. Once they were inside, Bobby went one way while Nick and Mike went another.

"Nice place," Nick said as they wandered around the club looking for Hector.

"Yeah, it is a nice club. It almost burned down in the mid-nineties," Mike said over the music. They went out to the open-air part of the club, which was under a thatched roof.

"How you know so much about this place?"

"I came here few times with Nina before I knew she was married to Hector." Mike paused. "She really liked this place."

"You really liked Nina, didn't you?" Nick said.

"There was something special about her."

Out on the patio, the place pounded with a mix of new and old salsa. The crowd ranged from the thirty-something crowd to South American teenagers. There were even a few older couples. But Hector wasn't out there, so they went back inside. That's when Mike saw her coming out of the VIP room.

He stood and watched her walk through the club and make her way to the bar. Mike tapped Nick on the shoulder. "There she is."

"Who?" Nick asked.

"Nina." Nick turned around quickly. "Wait here," Mike said as Bobby walked up.

"I don't see Hector anywhere," Bobby said to Nick.

"He's here." Nick pointed toward the bar where Mike was now standing next to Nina.

"Hello, Nina," Mike said.

PAYBACK

Nina closed her eyes and allowed her head to drift back at the sound of his voice. "Hello, Black," she said without looking at him. "What are you doing here?"

"I'm looking for Hector."

"I was hoping you'd say something noble like you came here looking for me. That you couldn't live another minute without seeing me."

"It is good to see you, Nina, even if you won't look at me." Nina took a deep breath and turned around slowly. "You look good, Nina."

"So do you. Very good."

"Where's Hector?" Mike asked before the conversation went in another direction.

"He's in the VIP room. But if you stand here and talk to me long enough, he'll be out here soon. I'm sure somebody will run and tell him that I'm out here talking to this big, fine black man," Nina said and put her hand on Mike's chest.

"I wanna talk to him, Nina." Mike slowly removed her hand from his chest. "Not have to kill him over you."

Nina looked at the ring on Mike's finger. "You're married?"

"Happily."

"Now that were both married, maybe you'll come down here to see me."

"I still don't mess with married women."

"Is that why you never came looking for me?"

"It's the only reason I didn't come and get you, Nina. If you weren't married to Hector . . ." Mike paused and looked around the club. "Who knows?"

"I do." Nina smiled a satisfied smile and turned around to motion for a waitress. When one responded,

Nina talked to her for a minute, then she returned her attention to Black. "Tell her what you want."

Mike reached in his pocket and handed the woman a hundred-dollar bill. "Tell Mr. Villanueva that Mike Black sends his respect and asks that Mr. Villanueva give him a minute of his time. Tell him exactly what I said. I'll be right here waiting for his answer."

The waitress was about to go to deliver the message, but Nina stopped her. "Wait until ten minutes after I'm back in the VIP before you come in there." Once the waitress was gone, Nina turned to Mike. "Goodbye, Black. I want to kiss you. I want you to hold me in your arms and kiss me, not just a goodbye kiss or a hug and a kiss on the cheek. I want you to kiss me the way that you used to." Nina took a step closer and ran her hand up Mike's crotch then whispered in his ear, "What I'd really like to do is suck that big dick and then ride you until I feel it swell up and explode inside me." And then Nina stepped away. "But then somebody would die tonight. Goodbye, Mike Black. I hope this won't be the last time I see you."

"You never know, Nina. Anything is possible."

"We'll see," Nina said and walked away.

Nick and Bobby joined Mike at the bar. Mike watched Nina as she made her way back to the VIP room. She didn't look back.

Nina looked exactly the way he remembered her. It was like time stood still for Nina. When they were involved with one another, Mike never knew that she was married, and definitely not that she was married to Hector. Nina never wore a ring, and he never asked her any questions. Mike never called her; he never even knew her number. She never knew his number.

PAYBACK

That was the way she wanted it. All spontaneous and natural, is what Nina used to call it.

When Mike saw Nina anywhere, anytime, he would drop whatever and whoever he was with to be with her. When they would get together, they had the best time. They even went on trips together. They went to Miami all the time, and to several islands. In his wildest dreams, he never imagined that Nina was married. But whenever they'd get back, Nina would leave and Mike wouldn't see her for a while. But he wanted to. There was something special about Nina.

Mike didn't find out she was married to Hector until he saw her one night on the street. They talked for a while then she said, "Oh shit, here comes my husband."

"You're married? To who?" Nina pointed at Hector then walked away without a word. Not too long after that, Hector shipped her down to Miami and Mike never saw her again.

"You all right, Black?" Nick asked.

"Yeah. I sent Hector a message."

"Yeah," Bobby said. "Nina is still fine as hell."

A half-hour later, Mike looked up and saw two men escorting Nina out of the VIP room. "Get ready."

"What's up?" Nick asked and put his hand on his gun, while Bobby turned toward Black.

Mike pointed as the two men pushed their way through the crowd and took Nina out of the club. "You know Hector wasn't gonna talk to me with Nina around. Probably took him this long to convince her to leave." Once Nina was safely out of the club, the two men approached Mike at the bar.

"Mr. Black?"

"Yes."

48

"Mr. Villanueva will see you now," one of the men said then turned toward the VIP room. Black, Bobby and Nick followed them.

Nick overheard one speak to the other in Spanish. "Debemos apenas los dirigió fuera espalda y los mata."

"No, permitió que ellos hablen primero entonces que nosotros los podemos matar."

Hearing their plans, Nick laughed. "Black."

"What they say?"

"One said they should just lead us out back and kill us. The other said, 'No, let them talk first, then we can kill them.' "

"Okay," Mike said. "So, now we know. Be ready."

Hector Villanueva sat alone in a booth in the VIP room, but one of his men stood next to him. As Mike approached, Hector extended his hand for him to sit down. "Mike Black."

"How are you, Hector?" Mike said as he sat down. Nick and Bobby stood on Black's side of the table, while Hector's men stood on the other. Bobby smiled, and the stare-down began.

"I am doing very well, Black. But I am curious. I thought that I made it very clear that I considered our business together concluded. Now here you are, and I want to know why. Why are you here?"

"My wife was kidnapped by two Latinos and a white guy at my club in the Bahamas earlier today. The bandits brought her by boat to Miami."

"And you think I had something to do with it?"

"No, Hector. I just wanna find my wife. This is your city. I was just hoping that you might have heard something."

PAYBACK

Hector sat back in the booth and finished his drink. It caught him off guard when Black asked for his help. It made him feel powerful. *Mike Black comes to me for help.* "I am very sorry to hear about your wife, Black, and very sorry that I can't help you, but I don't know anything about it. But if I hear anything, I will let you know."

"Thank you, Hector. I would appreciate that." Mike started to get up, but sat back down. "One more thing you can help me with, Hector."

"What is that, Black?"

"I overheard your boys saying that they were going to kill us after I talked to you. I don't think anybody needs to die tonight. I hope you agree."

Hector looked at Mike and then to his men. "Yes, I agree. Nobody needs to die tonight."

Mike stood up and extended his hand. "Thank you for taking the time to see me." He started to ask how Nina was doing just to fuck with Hector, but he decided against it.

Hector accepted Black's hand and stood up. "I am honored that you would come to me."

Once they were out of the club and in the car, Bobby asked, "Was all that really necessary? I'm about to throw up with all that touchy-feely, thank-you-for-seeing-me, honored-that-you-would-come-to-me shit."

"You never know when we might need an ally down here. Let's get back to New York. And besides," Mike paused as Bobby drove off, "I really came here to see Nina."

Chapter Seven

Freeze met them at JFK airport in New York at 10:30 that morning and drove them straight to Cuisine, a supper club that Mike owned. Their flight left Miami at 5:30, but they had an hour layover in Atlanta. During the flight, Nick and Bobby slept, while Mike looked out the window at the early morning sun above the clouds. As hard as he tried, he couldn't sleep.

The only thing on his mind was Shy. Was she all right? Who had her? Where were they taking her? If they were holding her for ransom, why no demand? Hundreds of possibilities and countless questions rolled around in his mind. When they arrived at Cuisine, they stopped at the bar before heading to what was now Freeze's office.

"Freeze," Mike said.

"Yo."

"Tell me what's up. Bitch-ass D-Train?" Mike asked, more to take his mind off Shy than anything else.

"Last couple of nights his people been postin' up in our spots. I thought he was smarter than that, to just roll up in our spots and set up shop. What they think I was gonna do? Nothin' they could do to avoid the consequences."

"He sees this as an opportunity. Me gone, Bobby layin' back, makes it look like your strength is exhausted. We need to deal with this now or other muthafuckas will raise up outta nowhere to try some shit like this."

"You knew sooner or later this was gonna happen. We had a long run. Peaceful," Bobby said, "everybody respectin' everybody's position and everybody making money. Muthafuckas ain't got no respect for shit."

"Don't be so hard on them, Bobby. That was us ten years ago. Young, not afraid of shit, we took power. We saw André slippin', layin' back, lettin' us run the show. Like we doin' now, me kickin' it in the Bahamas, you playin' the role. This was bound to happen sooner or later."

"See what you started when you killed Chilly, Nick?" Bobby asked, and Nick simply nodded his head. Before Nick killed him, Chilly ran most of the drugs uptown. He used to deal for André back in the day. It was Chilly who made peace with Mike, and they set up the dead zone where nobody would deal. Now D-Train was trying to step up to Chilly's position by moving on the dead zone.

"What do we do now? Freeze asked. Whether Mike intended to or not, he made Freeze feel like this was happening because somebody, maybe everybody saw him as weak; somebody they could roll over. He knew that whatever happened from this point forward, he would have to take the lead, step up and crush this nigga quick.

"The thing to do now is figure out what your enemies are plannin' and stop them. The next thing to do, and hopefully you have, is prevent any more of his people from tryin' to set up in our houses."

"We need to start takin' the shit to them, Black. He set up in Rocky's old spot," Freeze recommended.

"Just fall up in there and start blastin'?" Bobby asked.

"We used to," Mike said. The timing of this wasn't lost on him. This couldn't be happening at a worse time. What he should have been doing was concentrating his attention, his efforts, and his power on fighting off the takeover bid, but he couldn't. All his resources were tied up in finding Shy. His enemy would know that and exploit it. A smart enemy would make it happen.

As Nick and Freeze went to the office, Mike and Bobby continued the conversation. "I remembered reading once that it is only one who is thoroughly acquainted with the evils of war that can understand the profitable way of conducting it."

"And the best thing is to take over our operation intact. Destroying it isn't the smart move," Bobby said.

"Exactly my point, Bobby. That ain't Curl. On his best day he wouldn't have the brains to try this. He wouldn't see the profit in it. You want somebody to kick in some doors, do some killin' and be brutal about it, Curl's your man, but not like this." Mike paused. "Somebody is pullin' his strings. That's who our enemy is."

When Mike and Bobby came in the office, they found Freeze on the phone, nodding his head, and

PAYBACK

Nick seated comfortably on the couch. Freeze looked at Mike and then to Nick.

"Who was on the phone?"

"Angelo. He says he needs to see you as soon as you can. Says it important."

"He say what it was about?"

"Nick."

Chapter Eight

"Tony no!" Shy shouted.

Seeing the police open fire on Tony and watching as he fell to the ground, Shy took a deep breath. She tossed and turned. "Tony's dead." She was having a nightmare. "This way, Shy!" She saw Orlando die.

"Freeze!"

The cop fired.

Shy tried to sit up, but she couldn't. It had been a long time since she had nightmares about the night Tony died and she became a fugitive. Now she lay blindfolded and spread-eagle on a bed, with her hands and legs tied. Shy had no idea where she was or how she got there. The last thing she remembered was being on the boat with Sal and Julio when the doctor came. Then Sal held her while the doctor gave her a sedative.

Shy moved her eyebrows up and down, trying to move her blindfold enough so she could see. All she could tell was that she was in a small room and that the sun was shining. Nothing more.

PAYBACK

All Shy could do now was wait. Wait to see what was going to happen next. *Am I being held for ransom? Are they gonna kill me? Or rape me and then kill me?* Shy tried to think of something a bit more pleasant. She thought about the trip she and Mike took to Rio. Not only about the wonderful time they had there, but also about how, in Rio de Janeiro, Shy first started talking about facing her charges.

It began one night after the club closed. Shy began talking about the Bahamian celebration of Carnival.

"But do you know what I've always wanted to do?" Shy asked as she sat down at one of the tables.

"What's that?"

"I wanna go to Carnival in Rio."

"You've never been to Carnival in Rio de Janeiro, Cassandra?" Mike said, trying to sound as bougie and superior as he could.

Shy rolled her eyes at him and said in the same tone. "No, Michael, I've never been to carnival in Rio de Janeiro."

"Neither have I. And I always wanted to go there, too," Mike said and sat next to her. "Only reason I haven't gone is I don't wanna be bothered with the crowds."

"I know what you mean." Shy paused and thought for a second. "Well, why don't we go for a few days and leave before the crowds come?"

"That's fine, but it does kinda kill the purpose in going if we leave before Carnival."

Shy leaned forward, looked into his eyes and smiled. "So, do you think you can tolerate the crowds for a day or two?"

"How can I say no to those eyes and that smile?"

a story by roy glenn

Shy paused and thought for a moment. "I got a better idea. Why wait for Carnival? Why don't we just go?" she asked. "I don't know about you, but I could really use a couple of days off this rock."

Now it was Mike who paused, then he smiled at his wife. "Sounds like a real plan coming together."

"Perfect!" Shy said. "There's one more thing," Shy said and moved her chair closer to his. "And I know how you feel about it, but can we, you know, like, play tourist?"

Mike took a deep breath and agreed, even though his idea of the perfect vacation was to be as far away from other people as possible. Sightseeing required being around a bunch of people that Mike didn't want to be bothered with. On the other hand, Shy was desperate to be around people, to be a part of the crowd.

Shy missed being in New York, missed being a part of the whole *I live in New York* experience. Living on an island paradise was wonderful, but it does get old after a while. There were times when Shy wondered how Mike could stand it. *But he goes to New York at least two or three time a month,* Shy would rationalize. There were many days when she'd seen Mike get up early, catch a flight to New York and be back late that night.

When Mike woke up the following morning, Shy was at the computer and had arranged the entire trip. She informed him that she had chartered a plane, and they were staying at the Copacabana Palace Hotel, a five-star hotel on the beach. She told him that she had arranged for them to take a tour of the top ten attractions in Rio.

"Like what?" Mike asked.

PAYBACK

"It's a lotta stuff in Portuguese that I really can't pronounce, but trust me, I know how fascinated you are by historical things, so I know you'll love it," Shy assured him.

As soon as they landed, Shy grabbed the first brochure that she could find and began to read aloud to Mike. "Rio de Janeiro is the name of both a state and a city in southeastern Brazil," a very excited Shy read as she eased her arm around Mike's. "The city is famous for the hotel-lined tourist beaches, one of which we're staying at, Copacabana, and Ipanema, for the giant statue of Jesus, known as Cristo Redentor or something like that. But it means *Christ the Redeemer.* It's on the Corcovado Mountain, which, by the way, is part of our tour tomorrow. It's Brazil's second-largest city after São Paulo and used to be the country's capital until 1960, when Brasília took its place."

"Fascinating."

The first day Shy and Mike wandered around, Shy shopped and took pictures with her new digital camera. As it turned out, Shy was right about her husband. Mike found Rio de Janeiro to be a city rich with history and magnificent architecture, both of which fascinated him. Now as they walked back to their hotel, it was Mike reading from a guidebook aloud to Shy. "The actual city wasn't founded until March 565 by Portuguese knight Estácio de Sá, who called it São Sebastião do Rio de Janeiro, which means St. Sebastian of the January River, in honor of King Sebastian of Portugal. It was frequently attacked by pirates, especially enemies of Portugal, such as the Netherlands and France. In the late 16th century, the Portuguese crown began treating the village as a strategic location for Atlantic transit of ships between

Brazil, the African colonies, and Europe. Fortresses were built and an alliance was formed with nearby native tribes to defend the settlement against invaders," Mike read.

Shy kissed Mike on the cheek. "See, baby, I told you you'd love it."

"You were right, I do. Just like I love you."

"I love you too. And I just love being in a real city," Shy said and moved on quickly. "What do you want to eat?"

"Something Brazilian. Seafood is always nice," Mike replied and Shy broke out her list of recommended restaurants.

"What about Confeitaria Colombo? According to the map it's not far from here."

"I thought we passed that while we were downtown," Mike said.

"This is a branch of the one downtown. It's located at the Copacabana Fort, and it says that it offers the most beautiful view of Copacabana Beach."

And with that thought in mind, Shy requested a table outside. They were escorted to their table, and Mike pulled her chair out for her. *Always the perfect gentleman.*

After the waiter took their order, Shy looked out at the sand and the water, felt the gentle breeze against her cheeks. One thing she couldn't deny, she loved the beach.

As promised, they went sightseeing the following day. Their first stop was Corcovado. There they found Rio´s best-known icon, Cristo Redentor, Christ the Redeemer, a concrete statue of 30 meters whose wide open arms seemed to embrace the city and offered a magnificent view of Rio.

Mike had to admit, "The view is spectacular, Cassandra. I am glad you talked me into this."

After a day of sightseeing, they had a late dinner at Tia Palmira, which served extremely fresh fish, shrimp or crab all prepared with typical Brazilian recipes. They started with fried squid and then a bobó de camarão, which is shrimp in palm oil and ground yucca. "I love it here," Shy said while they waited for their food.

"Do you really? Maybe we could have moved here."

"That would be fine except that I don't speak Portuguese. But I love it. I love being in a city, any city." Then Shy paused. "Don't you wanna move back to New York?"

"No."

"I do."

"You ready to go to jail?" Mike asked, as he did every time Shy mentioned New York. But he wasn't prepared for her answer.

"Yes."

"What?"

"I said yes. Living on an island paradise is wonderful, and I love being there with you. I love being anywhere that you are." Shy reached across the table and held Mike's hands. "Michael, I love you, but I am bored out of my mind in the Bahamas."

"Okay, so we'll pick another island."

"You're not understanding me, Michael. I want to go back to New York, and I'm willing to go to jail if I have to," Shy said slowly and clearly, making sure that she pronounced every syllable.

"Have you lost your mind?"

"No, baby, I really am thinking about it. What I'm hoping is that I won't have to do any time, and if I do, it won't be for long. I've been talkin' to Wanda, and she thinks she can plea it down to a misdemeanor and get probation, or I may only have to do a year."

"No," Mike said flatly and Shy dropped it. She was enjoying their vacation too much to ruin it with that.

They had fun the next couple of days, spending their days either at the beach or somewhere near the water and sightseeing. Their nights were spent dancing at clubs like the Nova Lounge and Spazio in Ipanema. The subject didn't come up again during the rest of the trip, but it was all out there.

They didn't discuss it again until the night before all this began, Shy was thinking when she heard somebody unlocking the door. She tried to lie as still as possible and watched as two people entered the room. All that Shy could see under the blindfold was that it was a man and woman.

"There she is. You happy now?" Shy heard the man say.

"No. I'd be happy if you kill the bitch now and get it over with," the woman said.

"That ain't gonna happen. I told you before, the man says to keep her alive until he gets here."

"You could say that she was trying to escape and you had to shoot her."

"What you think I'ma do? Untie her, tell her to run and shoot her in the back? Is that what you think I should do? Do I look stupid to you? 'Cause that's how that move would make me look—stupid, stupid and dead."

"I don't care what you tell them, just kill her."

PAYBACK

"Ain't happenin'."

Shy watched as the woman stepped closer to the man. "Please, baby. Do it for me."

"I told you that shit ain't happenin', now stop fuckin' asking me that shit. This bitch gonna lay right here, *alive,* until he gets here and takes her off my hands."

The man and woman left the room, but before they closed the door, Shy heard the man say, "I thought you was over that shit."

As Shy heard the door lock, she tried to think of who this woman was and why she wanted the man to kill her so badly.

Chapter Nine

There weren't too many days when Detective Kirkland was late getting to the precinct, but today was one of those days. It was a little after 12:30 when Kirk sat down at his desk with his coffee. And it wasn't too much longer before he heard, "Kirk! You and Richards, my office now!"

"What did you do now?" Kirk asked Richards as he got up.

"I ain't did shit, officer. That bitch trippin'," Richards joked as he followed Kirk into the captain's office, where there were two men already seated in front of the captain's desk. The two men rose to their feet when the detectives entered the office. Kirk recognized one of them right away.

"Detectives, this is State Senator Martin Marshall, and this is Kenneth DeFrancisco of the DEA," the captain said, and the men all shook hands. "Kirk here is our resident expert on Mike Black."

PAYBACK

"What can you tell me about Mike Black's involvement in drug trafficking, detective?" Agent DeFrancisco asked.

"Nothing," was Kirk's simple answer.

"Excuse me?" The agent gave the captain a puzzled look then looked back at Kirk.

"I can't tell you anything because there's nothing to tell. Mike Black has no involvement in drugs or drug trafficking."

"We have information that leads us to believe that's incorrect," Senator Marshall said.

Kirk looked at Marshall, making no effort to hide his contempt. "And what might that be?"

"We'll share that information with you at the appropriate time, detective," Agent DeFrancisco answered. "Right now, what I need is your assistance in this investigation."

"I assured the agent that you would assist the DEA in any way you could, detective," the captain interjected.

"You planning on conducting this investigation in the Bahamas, Agent DeFrancisco? 'Cause that's where he is."

"Mr. Black and two associates arrived at JFK at ten-thirty this morning," Marshall said.

"Now, you two will serve in primarily an advisory role, but I'm sure you'll get in on some of the action," Agent DeFrancisco said and stood up. "Captain, I'll leave you to brief the detectives. Thanks for your time and cooperation." Agent DeFrancisco and Senator Marshall left the office.

After they were gone, Kirk asked the captain, "Now, what the fuck was that about, Gus? You know as well as I do that Black's got nothing to do with drugs."

"That's true as far as I know, but who knows?"

"And to be honest with you, I don't trust anything that that sleaze Marshall is involved in."

"Look, Kirk, the guy is a state senator, and that means I don't fuck with him unless it is absolutely necessary." The captain handed Kirk a piece of paper. "Listen, you and Richards report to that address in the morning. You spend a couple months with those assholes, tellin' them what they wanna know, and if you're lucky, maybe you'll get to spend some time in the Bahamas."

"I'm all for that," Richards said.

"Okay, Gus," Kirk said and stood up. "But I still don't like it."

"Yeah, whatever, enjoy the vacation. Check with Narcotics before you go. Make sure that what these assholes are doing doesn't interfere with any on-going operations."

"Yes, sir," Kirk said and left the captain's office.

Kirk and Richards went straight to the head of Narcotics, Lieutenant Gene Sanchez. "You're wasting your time, Kirk. We got nothing goin' on Black. The guy's been off our radar for years," Sanchez told Kirk.

"What about his wife, Cassandra Sims? Got anything on her?"

"She never was a major player. We had to drop the murder case against her, and her lawyer's been putting a lot of pressure on the ADA to produce some evidence. We lack evidence and we have no witnesses. Half the people that were there are dead, and the ones that didn't die are doing their time quietly, so sooner or later we'll be forced to drop our conspiracy to distribute case against her. So, if the fuckin' DEA got something on either one of them, you make damn sure they fuckin' share it with me."

"You know I will," Kirk said, and he and Richards got ready to leave.

"Wait a minute. There is one thing."

"What's that, Sanchez?"

"The last couple of weeks we been hearing rumbles of a war brewing between his boy Freeze and D-Train Washington."

"Who's he?" Richards asked.

"He took over what's left of Chilly's crew."

"What's the beef over?"

"Chilly's people trying to roll in their so-called dead zone. We're on top of it."

"That's one more reason why this doesn't make sense."

"What's that, Kirk?"

"These guys have protected that dead zone like it was the holy fuckin' grail for years."

"That's true," Sanchez had to agree.

"Now all of a sudden Black wants back in the drug game? Why now?"

"Maybe that's why Simmons killed Chilly, so they could take over Chilly's business," Richards said.

"It's possible," Sanchez said.

"Come on, Pat, you arrested him. You know Simmons was fuckin' Chilly's wife and the animal found about it. That's why Simmons killed Chilly," Kirk told Sanchez. "And besides, Black gave Chilly that spot."

"What are you talkin' about?" Richards wanted to know.

"You should teach the kid some history, Kirk," Sanchez said and walked toward the window. "What's it been, Kirk? Ten, twelve years?"

"About that."

"The story goes, the night Black caught up with Vincent Martin and his crew, it was him, Bobby Ray and Freeze. They walked in blastin' and killed them all, except one guy. Black walks up to the guy and says tell Chilly to come see him," Sanchez explained.

"After that, there's the dead zone," Kirk said. "And Chilly respected that shit for years."

"But Chilly's dead, and D-Train wants to step up," Richards said.

"Right. It's a good move for D-Train to move on the dead zone," Kirk said.

"Okay, okay," Sanchez said. "That explains why D-train would want to go to war, but what's in it for Black? He didn't have to kill Chilly or take on this other clown to get back in the drug game. He got an organization already in place. And if that was happening, I would know about it, Kirk."

Kirk stood up and headed for the door. "That's why this makes no sense."

Chapter Ten

"Nick?" Mike asked. "What does Angelo want to talk to me about Nick for?"

"I don't know, Black. When I asked him what it was about, all he said was *Nick* and hung up the phone," Freeze said as Nick came into the office.

"All right, let's go see what Angee wants." Mike stood up and started for the door, followed by Nick and Freeze.

"Hey, Mike, I got some business that I need to handle," Bobby said, and Freeze shot him a look. "It's not going to take me long. Couple of hours at most."

"Handle your business," Mike said.

"I'll get with you later," Bobby said.

After Bobby left the office, Freeze leaned toward Black. "Remind me to tell you something about Bobby," he said, and they left the office.

Mike had Freeze drive him and Nick to Yonkers to see Angelo Collette. They pulled up in front of a small private club and were met at the curb by two large gentlemen. Jimmy Lacoursiere and his associate approached the car as Mike and Nick got out of the car. "You comin', Freeze?" Mike asked as he and Nick followed Jimmy inside the club.

"Yeah, I'll be in there in a minute. I just need to check on something."

"Cool." Once they were inside, Mike turned to Jimmy. "Jimmy, how are you?" Mike said, handing Jimmy his guns.

"I'm okay, Black." He patted down Mike. "Angelo's in the back. He's waiting for you."

Mike went down the hall to Angelo's office and knocked on the door.

"Come on in, Mikey, and sit down.

"How's it goin', Angee?"

"A little older, a little smarter," Angelo said. "What about you, Mikey?"

"I don't know if you know it or not, but somebody kidnapped Cassandra from my club in the Bahamas yesterday."

"No, Mikey, I didn't know that. Tell me, what I can do?"

"You can take me to the guy that did it. His name is Sal."

"Shit, Mikey, you know how many guys call themselves Sal? Like lookin' for a fuckin' needle in a fuckin' haystack."

"This one used to run with two Latinos, but they're both dead. They were meeting an undercover DEA agent yesterday."

"At your spot?"

"Yeah," Mike said as he stepped to the bar and poured himself a drink. "Shit went south for them, and

69

they ended up clippin' the agent and takin' Cassandra."

"Do you remember Sally Fitz?

"Yeah, I remember him. Why?"

"Sal made a reputation for himself for being able to get anything for anybody, as long as they could pay his price. This naturally makes Sally very popular in some circles. I know he's been workin' with a couple Cubans. I don't know if he's in New York, or where to find him."

"If he's my guy and he's in New York, I'll find him," Mike said confidently. "Now, what did you want to see me about?"

"Nick."

"What about Nick?"

"Nick's made some people very upset lately."

"Who?"

"Diego Estabon." Before Chilly met his untimely demise, Diego Estabon used to supply him.

"Diego?" Mike had known Diego Estabon for a very long time. He used to do business with Diego's father, Gomez, back when Black was an enforcer. He respected Gomez, but had none for Diego. "What's he pissed about?"

"Diego says Nick is DEA."

"Nick?"

"Nick," Angelo answered.

"That's bullshit, Angee. Nick ain't the DEA. I'm not buying that shit."

"He said Nick cost him a lot of money."

"I don't need this, Angee, not now."

"Said Nick did a lot of damage to his operation. On top of that, Nick killed Chilly, and you know Chilly was making big money for him."

"What does Diego expect? Chilly came to kill Nick 'cause he fucked Chilly's wife."

"Nick fucked Gee?" Angelo asked and Mike nodded his head. "Gee's a bad bitch. I woulda fucked her fine ass too."

"Fuckin' with married women is bad for business."

"Whatever, Mikey. He said Nick killed some guy named Felix and some general. Diego says they were an important part of his operation."

"The General was Nick's commander in the Army. After they got them out of South America, Felix recruited what was left of his team. Nick went after them after they had his partner, Jett, killed and tried to kill the other partner. She's still in the hospital now. But Nick didn't kill Felix and the General."

"He didn't?"

"Freeze killed them."

"What difference does it make, Mikey? The fuckers are still dead."

"Okay, so what does he want?"

"Nick. He wants Nick."

"I can't believe that Nick is DEA."

"It don't matter what you believe. The question is, is he or isn't he?"

Mike sat back and thought about it. Whether he wanted to believe it or not, the possibility did exist. Nick could be a DEA operative, and if that were true, he would have to be dealt with.

"What does Diego want?"

"He wants to sit down with you."

"When and where?"

"The where is here. I'll call you when he calls me."

Mike stood up. "Let me know."

PAYBACK

Once they were outside and heading for the car, Mike looked at Freeze. "Nick, you drive," he said, and Freeze nodded his head. Freeze threw Nick the keys to his truck and got in the back seat on the driver's side.

As Nick drove away, Mike sat in the front seat and thought about what Angelo had told him. Suddenly the DEA was all up in everything. First a DEA agent was killed in his club, now Angelo said Nick was DEA. Coincidence? Maybe. Nick did say he knew the agent who was killed in Black's Paradise, so it was possible they could have been working together.

Even if it were true, why would he involve Cassandra?

Mike looked at Nick and refused to believe that somebody he'd known most of his life would turn on him. But like it or not, believe it or not, Mike had to face it and do it now. "Hey, Nick, do you remember when you and Jamaica had that scam goin' where y'all were shakin' down the number runners that you knew were skimmin' money off André?"

"Yeah, that was a sweet hustle while it lasted," Nick said as he drove. He didn't notice that Freeze had taken out his gun and set it on his lap.

"André was pretty lax about that whole gambling thing, wasn't he?" Mike asked.

"Yeah, all André saw was drug money. The houses, the women, the numbers, none of that made any difference to him. It wasn't until you took over that the money got right."

"Yeah, but it fucked up y'all's hustle. And I know you and Jay were makin' crazy money off them muthafuckas, right?"

"Damn sure was, Black."

72

"But when I took that shit over, you came to me like a man and told me about it. I didn't even have to ask you. You just came to me and said, 'Yo Black, this what's happenin', boom, boom, boom.' Even though that shit cost you money."

"Come on, Black. I was loyal to you and you trusted me."

"Are you still loyal to me, Nick? Can I still trust you, Nick?"

Nick looked at Mike. "Of course I am."

"Nick, I gotta ask you something. Something important. I don't even like having to ask you some shit like this, but I gotta."

"What you wanna ask me, Black?"

"Are you DEA?"

Before he answered the question, Nick glanced in the rearview mirror at Freeze. Nick immediately pulled off to the side of the road and put the car in park.

"Why you ask me that, Black?" Mike didn't answer. "No! Hell fuckin' no, I am not DEA."

"Tell me why Diego Estabon thinks you are?"

"Diego?" Nick said excitedly. He couldn't believe what he was hearing. "I don't know, but it might be because it was his plant we were moving on in South America when most of our unit got killed. Maybe it's because he had Jett killed and he's the reason Monika is in the hospital. Maybe it's because I killed Chilly."

"And Felix and the General," Mike pointed out.

"I killed them, Black," Freeze said.

"Diego says you cost him a lot of money."

"Look, Black, I swear to you, I am not the fuckin' DEA."

"I had to ask."

73

PAYBACK

Nick looked at Mike and glanced in the back seat at Freeze. "You were gonna kill me behind some shit fuckin' Diego Estabon said?"

"No, Nick, I wasn't gonna kill you on his word. But I had to look into your eyes and ask you that question," Mike said and looked back at Freeze. Nick turned back to Freeze.

"Yeah, Nick, I'da killed you. It wouldn't be easy, much shit as we been through, but yeah, I woulda done it."

Nick looked at Mike. "It's cool, Nick. I believe you," Mike said and Nick drove off. He never really believed Nick was DEA.

No, Diego is working some other angle, Mike thought.

"Do you remember Sally Fitz?" he asked Nick.

"Yeah, I remember him. But if you're thinkin' it's the same Sal, I doubt it. I woulda recognized him," Nick said.

"Freeze, I know that you got shit you need to handle, but you and Nick ask around, see if you can find Sally Fitz," Mike told them. "Angee says Sally Fitz is workin' with two Cubans. And two Latinos and a white guy named Sal kidnapped Cassandra. Too much of a coincidence."

"Even if it is just a coincidence, Sally Fitz knows a lot of people. He might able to put us on to something. 'Cause right now we ain't got shit," Freeze said.

Chapter Eleven

While Nick and Freeze went to find Sally Fitz, Mike sat impatiently at Cuisine, waiting for Bobby to return. It was at that point that he remembered Freeze said he needed to talk to him about Bobby.

After about a half-hour of waiting, Mike finally picked up the phone and called Bobby on his cell phone. On the fourth ring, a female voice tentatively answered.

"Sorry," Mike said. "I must have the wrong number."

As he was about to hang up the phone, the female said, "You wanna talk to Bobby?"

"Yes," a confused Mike answered.

"Hold on."

In the background, Mike could hear her whispering, "Bobby, Bobby, wake up. Bobby, come on. Bobby, wake the fuck up, nigga," she said a little louder. "I think it's Black on the phone."

A half-asleep Bobby took the phone. "Hello."

PAYBACK

"I'm at Cuisine, man, waiting for you. What the fuck are you doin'?"

"Huh."

"What the fuck are you doin'?" Mike said louder.

"Mike?"

"Yeah. I'm at Cuisine waiting for you. What the fuck are you doin', man?"

"Damn, I'm on my way," Bobby said quickly and hung up the phone before Mike got a chance to at least ask him how long he would be.

Thirty minutes later, Bobby burst into the office at Cuisine. "You ready?"

"I was ready an hour ago."

"Where are we goin'?"

"Let's just ride. I need to get out of here. I can't just sit here and do nothing," Mike said as he got up and followed Bobby out of the office.

Once they were in Bobby's car, Mike asked, "You wanna tell me about it, or you gonna make me ask?"

"Tell you about what, Mike?"

"Who was that woman answering your phone, and how did she know that it was me callin' you?" Mike asked, knowing that this was probably what Freeze wanted to tell him about.

"Her name is Cat."

"That's it? Her name is Cat? This Cat woman, whoever the fuck she is, is answering your fuckin' phone while you're sleeping, Bob. And all you got to say is her name is Cat?"

"Okay, okay, she a friend of mine."

"No shit. You fuckin' her?"

Bobby looked at Mike in silent response.

"You fuckin' around on Pam?"

Once again, Bobby's response was silent.

"I don't believe it. After all these years, you fuckin' around on Pam." Mike looked at Bobby, shaking his head.

"What?" Bobby said as he drove. "You gonna sit there and tell me that you ain't fuckin' any of those island hoes"

"No."

"Get the fuck outta here. All them fine-ass Bahamian bitches—and the tourists, let's not forget about the tourists—coming up in your spot, all tanned and topless, and you gonna tell me that you ain't fuckin' none of them?"

"No. The last woman that I fucked, other than my wife, was Melinda."

"Get the fuck outta here. Or has Melinda been down to the island?"

"No, Bobby, she hasn't been to the island, at least not that I know of."

"I didn't think so. She's been fuckin' around with Curl these days."

"Curl? She's fuckin' that nigga?" *Coincidence?*

"I guess she's just a gangster's girl," Bobby said with a laugh.

"What's up with that bitch-ass gangster anyway? You don't think that somebody must be backin' him up?"

"Since Nick killed Chilly, D-Train grew some balls and finally left 205th Street."

"You don't think that's a little strange?"

"Maybe it's Melinda backin' him up," Bobby joked. "Maybe she's pissed off that you dumped her for Shy, and this is her revenge."

PAYBACK

Mike laughed along with him. "I don't think so. That's a great combination, no balls and no brains."

Bobby's cell phone rang. "What's up?" Bobby answered.

"I need to see you," Cat said.

"I told you I got something to do. I'll get with you later."

"I know what you said, but I need to see you now. Just come by here. You fell asleep and didn't finish what you started."

Bobby's cell beeped with a call on the other line. He looked at the display. "Look, I got another call coming. I'll get with you later," he said and clicked to the other line. "What's up?"

"Bobby, this is Angelo. Is Mikey with you?"

"He's right here, Angelo, " Bobby said and handed Mike the phone.

"What's up?"

"Got a tip for you."

Chapter Twelve

Nick and Freeze rolled out of Cuisine and hit the streets. While Nick drove, Freeze made some calls. They checked a few places, but hadn't come up with anything. There was very little conversation between the two until Nick turned to Freeze and broke the silence. "You really woulda killed me, wouldn't you?"

"Yeah, Nick. I woulda put a bullet in the back of your head," Freeze replied nonchalantly.

"Like it wasn't shit," Nick said angrily, but what he was feeling inside was something different.

"Shit ain't changed, and I ain't either. I'd feel really bad about the shit, Nick, but yeah, if Black wanted you dead," Freeze said and stopped.

"I know," Nick said. He understood, but it still hurt.

"There's some shit you gotta realize. You been gone a long time. And when you do come back, you're still into the same shit, government shit that you were into before you got out. Only thing changed was you had a new master. All that time nobody hears from you until

PAYBACK

Gee set you up to be the fall guy for whatever her and her sister had cooked up for Chilly."

"I called Black a few times when I got back, but we never hooked up."

"Fuck that shit, Nick! I ain't hard to find. You shoulda came to see me!" Freeze yelled.

"You know what was up with that," Nick yelled back. "And why didn't you tell me what was up with Camille? You knew what was goin' on. Everybody knew! Everybody but me."

"I couldn't tell you nothin'. I had to check you out, see if you could be trusted."

"That why you helped me? So you could watch me? To see if I could be trusted?"

"No, Nick, I helped you 'cause you my nigga, my nigga from way back. You said you needed me to ride."

"Do you trust me?"

"If I didn't trust you, Nick, I'da killed you a long time ago and none of this would be happenin'," Freeze said, reminding Nick that this all began when one of the Latino men that came to Black's Paradise looked at him.

He must have recognized me, Nick thought, because the Latino immediately stood up and looked directly at him, took out his gun and shot the DEA agent in the head. Since then, Nick had been trying to remember where the man would have known him from and what was the connection to DEA agent Roman Patterson.

By 9:30, Freeze found out where Sally Fitz had been hanging out lately, and they were on their way to see him. When Nick and Freeze fell up in a place called Some Joint in Queens, they were glad they were both heavily armed. Nick spotted Sal at the bar, surrounded by four women, talking loud, drink in one hand, money in the other. There was never anything low profile about Sally Fitz.

"There he is."

"I see him," Freeze said. "And look, those must be the two Cubans Angelo told Black about."

"You watch them. I'm goin' over there," Nick said and made his way toward him. "Yo, Sal, Sally Fitz!"

He looked around to see who called him Sally Fitz. He only let certain people call him that. "Nick!" he yelled over the music.

His real name was Salvatore Fitzpatrick; his father was Irish and his mother was Italian. He and Nick did some work together when Sally Fitz used to run with Angelo. Their lives took a similar turn when he joined the Army. Only difference was Sally Fitz joined because he'd killed somebody, while Nick joined after Bobby tried to kill him.

Sally Fitz was the type of guy was always had a deal going. The last time Nick saw Sally Fitz was in Istanbul, Turkey. He was trying to sell some weapons back to the guys he'd stolen them from.

"Is that fuckin' Nick?" he yelled. He came toward Nick and shook his hand. "Good to see you, Nick. What you doin' in here?"

"Lookin' for you."

"For me? You didn't fall up in this joint by yourself, did you?"

"And suppose I did?" Nick looked around the room. "I can drop every ass in this joint if I had to."

"I fuckin' know you can, Nick. I fuckin' know you can."

"Don't worry about it, Sal. Freeze is with me."

PAYBACK

"Freeze! Shit, I haven't seen his ass in years. Where's he at?"

"Over there." Nick pointed at Freeze.

Sally Fitz threw up his arms. "Call him over."

"He's watchin' my back."

"This sounds fuckin' serious."

"Someplace quiet we can talk, Sal?"

"Outside. Come on." Nick followed Sally Fitz, and Freeze followed them both out of the club. The two Cubans followed Freeze. Sally Fitz walked across the street and waved for Freeze to join them. Once again, Freeze declined Sally Fitz's invitation, choosing instead to keep his eye on the two Cubans, who stood twenty feet away.

"So, what's up, Nick?" Sally Fitz asked.

"I'm lookin' for a guy named Sal that hangs out with a couple of Latinos."

Sally Fitz looked at the Cubans. "Seems like you found him," he answered.

"Not you, Sal. The Sal I'm looking for kidnapped Mike Black's wife yesterday in the Bahamas."

"That definitely ain't me. And if Black thinks it's me, you make sure you tell him that I didn't have shit to do with it. Me and him go too far back, Nick. Come on. Me, you, Angelo and Black, back in the day, fuckin' forget about it. I would never. You tell him that."

"I know, Sal. I was there when it happened, so I know it wasn't you. But you know people, Sal. I was hopin' that you knew the guy, since you both got the same name."

"Shit, Nick, you know how many guys there are named Sal?"

82

"Yeah, but like I said, this one hangs with two Latinos, probably South American."

Sally Fitz thought for a minute. "Now that you mention it, I think I do know who you're talkin' about. Sal Terrico. Does a lot of business south of the border."

"You know where I can find him?"

"I got no fuckin' idea. I only met the guy a few times. And for the life of me, I can't remember who it was that introduced us. Only reason I remember is 'cause we was both in the same place and somebody calls him and I answered. And that's been years ago."

"What does he look like?"

"Shit, I don't know. He's a tall, lanky guy, maybe six foot, black hair, mustache."

"Anything at all you could tell me about him?"

"All I can tell you about this guy is that he loves black chicks. He was with a different one every time I seen him. The guy was ravin' about how Queens had the best black strip clubs in the city, and how he been to all of them."

"He say what his favorite was?"

"Place called Cityscape or some shit like that."

"Thanks, Sal. You've been a big help," Nick said and started to walk away.

"Forget about it. I hope you get this guy. Hey, Nick, it's funny you come by 'cause I got something you might be interested in."

"What's that?"

"Really it's something you could do for me. You know a guy named Paris?"

PAYBACK

"Paris, yeah I know him. Considers himself an information broker. We did some business together. Why?"

"Yeah, well, he don't consider himself that no more, 'cause he's fuckin' dead."

"Who killed him?"

"One of his mules."

"Why'd the mule kill him?"

"Paris sent somebody to kill her, but his bitch kills him. So Paris sends two more guys after her. She whacks them. Then she shows up in LA and she puts a bullet in his brain."

"Just a regular Pam Grier, ain't she?"

"You know what I'm sayin'?"

"It's a colorful story, Sal, but why you tellin' me this shit?"

"When Paris sent the first guy after her, she was carryin' a package for him. The package was never recovered. And the buyer really wanted that package."

"And?"

"I don't know who the buyer was, but your pal General Peterson was brokering the deal."

"Now you got my attention. What was in the package?"

"The way I get it, it's got somethin' to do with South America and drugs."

Nick took a deep breath. He knew that the buyer had to be Diego Estabon. Both the General and Felix worked for him, so it made sense that he was the buyer. That would also explain Diego's interest in him. If he couldn't kill Nick, then maybe he could get Black to do it for him by accusing Nick of being DEA.

"You want something, Sal. What is it?"

"With Paris and the General both dead and the package still in the open, I figure a smart guy like me could step in and clean up. But I need what I'm looking for, so I was hopin' that since you was down there fuckin' around with the General, you might know something about it."

"Sorry, Sal, I can't help you," Nick lied. He had a good idea what was in those papers. There was probably enough information in them to get a lot of people in trouble for their involvement in the illegal drug eradication that Nick's unit was involved in. Diego was probably not the only one anxious to make those papers disappear, along with Nick and his partners, who could be called to testify if the truth ever surfaced in Washington.

"Good luck. I hope it works out for you." Without another word, Nick left Sally Fitz standing there.

As Freeze drove off, Nick told him what Sally Fitz told him about Sal Terrico. Freeze immediately called Black.

"I know," Black said. "We got a tip from Angelo. We're on our way there now."

"He likes the black tittie joints in Queens, but Cityscape is his favorite."

"You and Nick check that out. I'll call you later," Mike said.

"We're on it," Freeze said and turned to Nick. "We gotta check out that club," he said, but Nick didn't answer. "Nick, you all right, man?"

"Huh?"

"Black wants us to check out Cityscape."

"Okay," Nick replied, but his mind was still on Felix and the General and those missing papers. If those papers were still in the open and the buyer still wanted them, then Monika might still be in danger.

"Drive by the hospital, Freeze. I need to check on Monika."

Chapter Thirteen

On Angelo's word, Bobby drove out to Queens to a house on Maxwell Road. They both knew the place. It was known to be a shooting gallery, where a select clientele came to buy and shoot heroin. The place was run by a guy called Dirty Red. They called him that because of his long, red hair and beard, not to mention the fact that he was a dirty muthafucka. Some of Red's customers were important people who came there to get high in a safe and secure atmosphere.

Bobby parked the car, and he and Mike put on their gloves. They approached the house and knocked on the door. Mike took out his gun. One of Red's men opened the door. "Red here?" Bobby asked the huge man.

"Never heard of him."

PAYBACK

"Yeah, right," Mike said as he hit the man in the head with his gun.

"Heard of him now?" Bobby asked as the man fell to the floor. Then Bobby hit him again to be sure he was out cold.

Red heard the noise and came down the hall. "Black, Bobby, what are you doin' out here?" Red was a tall man, but he didn't weigh more than 185 pounds.

"We came for the same thing everybody else does. We came to see you, Red," Bobby said as he literally pushed his way past Red.

"I didn't know you guys were into this stuff. Well, since you're already in, what can I do for you?"

"We're lookin' for Sal Terrico," Bobby explained.

"Never heard of him," Red answered.

"Come on, Red," Bobby said. "Stop fuckin' around. We're lookin' for Sal Terrico. Is he here?"

"Look, I know people, important people," Red said.

"It was those people who sent us here," Bobby explained as Mike walked down the hall. He heard voices and saw a light coming from a room at the end of the hall.

"Whoa," Red said. "Slow down. You can't just come in here and start wandering around." Red walked up on Mike and reached for his shoulder, but before he could touch Mike, Bobby grabbed Red. He spun him around and grabbed Red's throat. "What the fuck are you doin'?" Red said, clutching his throat.

"You're not listening to me, Red," Bobby said. "And it hurts me." Bobby tightened his grip and Red gasped for air. "Now, let start again. We're lookin' for Sal Terrico."

While Bobby busied himself with Red, Mike reached the end of the hall. The room turned out to be

88

the kitchen. A man who looked very impatient and a woman holding a spoon over a candlelit flame were seated at the table. In front of her lay a thin rubber hose and a metal box with syringes in it.

"What took you so long, Red? Marge here is ready to fly. Aren't you, sweetie?" the man said and looked up to see that it was not Red, but Mike. "Hello," the man said.

"You should go," Mike said softly, and took his gun out of his pocket.

"What the—?"

"Now."

Both the man and the woman started to stand up. Mike looked at the woman. She was an attractive woman with long, blonde hair, very pretty eyes, and entirely too much makeup. "You stay. Finish what you were doin'."

"But that's mine. I paid for it," the man said. Mike looked at him. "Okay, okay, I'm going."

The man rushed out of the kitchen and down the hall past Bobby, who was still holding Red by the throat. "Bye-bye, sweetie," Bobby said. Once he was out, Bobby pushed Red into the kitchen, just as the woman finished filling a syringe with the heroin she'd been cooking. Mike held out his hand and she passed it to him.

"Now you can go."

With a very relieved look on her face, the woman quickly gathered her things. "So, I'll call you, Red."

As soon as the woman was gone, Bobby grabbed Red again. With one arm, Mike cleared everything from the table. Bobby threw Red down on the table and held him there. "We're looking for Sal Terrico. Is he here?" Bobby yelled.

"Fuck you, nigger. You can't just walk on in here and—" Red began to protest, but Mike punched him in the face.

"You don't want me to have to go room to room looking for him. If I do, most of your customers will never come back here. They'll find someplace else to shoot themselves to oblivion," Mike said as he stood over Red with the syringe in his hand.

"What you gonna do?" Red laughed. "Shoot me with my own shit?" Red pulled up his sleeve to reveal his track marks. "Go ahead! All I'll be is high! And I still ain't tellin' you shit!"

"Hold his head, Bobby."

Bobby grabbed Red by the throat with one hand and held his forehead with the other. Mike held his gun to Red's head and slowly moved the syringe toward Red's eye. "Who said I was gonna put it in your arm?" Mike inched the syringe closer.

Red tried to move his head, but Bobby's grip was too tight. The terror was apparent on Red's face as the syringe came close to his eye.

"Okay!"

Mike stopped. "Where is he?"

"Okay, he was here. But he's gone now."

"Was he alone?"

"No. He had some black chick with him."

Bobby looked at Mike. "What she look like?" he asked.

"She was tall for a chick, five-nine, maybe five-ten. Dark-skinned with long hair," Red gasped as Bobby tightened his grip on Red's throat.

"Was she all right?"

"Yes!" Red spit out. "She was all over him, beggin' him to hurry up and get it."

Mike looked at Bobby. Since he knew that Cassandra wasn't a shooter, Mike assumed it wasn't her. On top of that, it wouldn't make any sense at all for Sal to be riding around with her.

He was breathing hard, his heart was pounding. He wanted to kill Red. Mike knew that he needed to pull up. Red may become useful if Sal came back. "Sal, he come here a lot?" he asked.

"Whenever he's in town."

Mike moved his gun away from Red's head and threw the syringe on the floor. Bobby grabbed Red and pulled him up from the table. "If he comes here again, you call me at this number."

Chapter Fourteen

Bobby followed Mike out of the house, leaving Red clutching his throat and breathing hard. As soon as they were in Bobby's car, Mike called Freeze. "Where are you?"

"At the hospital."

"The hospital? What happened?"

"Everything's cool."

"Then what you doin' at the hospital?"

"I'll let Nick explain that to you," Freeze said as he watched Nick push Monika's wheelchair out of the hospital.

"Put him on."

"He can't talk right now. He's doin' what he gotta do."

"This about that girl that worked with him? What was her name?"

"Monika."

Mike held the phone and thought about what Freeze had told him about Nick's two partners. He said that while they were investigating Chilly, Monika had been shot five times. Two shots in the chest, two to the head, one hit her above the left ear. She caught one in her eye, and they weren't able to save the eye. The other one was in her hand. The next day, Nick found his other partner, Jett Bronson, dead with a trail of blood coming from his ear. "Tell him to call me," Mike said and hung up the phone.

As soon as he handed the phone back to Bobby the phone rang. Bobby looked at the number on the display, put the phone down, and started the car. "Where we goin' now?"

"Let's go check out Cityscape. It's a tittie bar on Queens Boulevard."

Bobby put the car in drive and wiped the sweat from his brow. "What's goin' on at the hospital?"

"Nick's taking care of some unfinished business. But fuck that for now. What I wanna know is what's up with this woman."

"Her name is Cat. I met her at Cynt's."

"What were you doin' at Cynt's?"

"You remember when Wanda was losing her mind about Freeze letting things run down at Cuisine and gettin' sloppy with everything else?"

"Yeah, what about it?"

"She asked me if I'd, you know, make the rounds, check up on him, see if shit was runnin' right."

"Okay."

"Freeze introduced me to her and she danced for me. Damn, that bitch can dance, and she was cool. I wasn't even tryin' to fuck her. We would just hang out, talk shit, that's it."

PAYBACK

"Yeah, right. You knew you were gonna end up fuckin' her when you started hangin' out with her," Mike said.

Bobby smiled. "She's a young girl, barely twenty-two, fine as hell; nice-sized titties, little bitty waist, with a toot-booty that can stop traffic. That body made her one of the most popular dancers at Cynt's."

"Young girl blow your mind."

Bobby paused before saying, "Yeah."

"So, you been hangin' out at Cynt's with this woman?"

"Not anymore. Cynt fired her for being late or not showing up at all."

"Was she with you when she was late or not showing up at all?"

"Yeah."

Mike started laughing. "You got the girl fired from her job, Bobby?"

Bobby laughed.

"Fuckin' up Cynt's business over some pussy? You know better than that," Mike said, continuing to laugh as Bobby's phone rang again. Bobby looked at the display, and once again he put the phone down without answering.

"That her?"

"Yeah," Bobby said louder than he needed to.

"She's kind of a pest, ain't she?"

Bobby shook his head. "Mike, you just don't know."

"If she's that much of a pest, why don't you cut her loose?"

"I tried, but she won't go."

"The fuck you mean, she won't go?"

a story by roy glenn

"She won't leave me alone. She'll call with some excuse to get me over there. Dumb shit, like she need a ride someplace or I got something of hers and she gotta have it right then."

"And you go?" Mike questioned.

"Yeah. I know what's gonna happen when I get there, but I do it anyway."

Mike looked at Bobby like he was a fool. "You're either a fool or you're pussy whipped."

"Pussy whipped. She'll always find a way to come out of her clothes or she'll just answer the door naked and I gotta fuck her. One time, she called me and said that she needed me to come get her from Cynt's 'cause she was locked out and needed to go to the Bowery to meet a friend of hers to get the keys," Bobby explained. "So I tell Pam that I gotta go make the rounds."

"Hold up," Mike interrupted. "What rounds? You ain't made rounds in years."

"Come on, Mike. Who does Pam talk to? She don't talk to Freeze, she thinks Wanda is overbearing, her and Shy are great friends, but only when they see each other." Bobby paused. "So I blamed it on you."

"What?"

"After that thing with Wanda and Freeze, I told her that you said I had to start making the rounds, you know, just to make sure things are goin' right. So when she calls, I tell Pam it's you reminding me that I need to make the rounds, 'cause you know I forget shit, especially shit I hate doin'."

"The old Bobby is back." Mike laughed. "You always were a lyin'-ass, pussy-gettin' muthafucka. I'm surprised you lasted so long. But let me ask you this.

PAYBACK

Why couldn't you just tell her you were goin' to the club?"

"She could call the club or just show up there. You know how she likes to just show up there. See, if I'm making the rounds, all she'll do is call my cell. I'd even call her from some of the houses."

"You were actually making the rounds and taking her with you."

"Yeah."

"How come I'm just hearin' about this?"

Bobby just looked at him.

"How long has this been goin' on?"

"Six, maybe seven months."

"You sportin' this bitch around with you for six months? Your ass was out of control." Mike laughed. "It's not that I give a fuck if you get some pussy. I'm just surprised, that's all. All these years you've been playing the happily married man with kids. You were the only faithful man I knew."

"Yeah, well, now you can be the only faithful man I know." Bobby laughed.

"What happened to all that shit about finding the right woman?"

"I did. I married her."

"You ain't thinkin' about leavin' Pam, are you?"

"No," Bobby said absolutely. "I would never leave Pam. I love her."

"Then what's up?"

"Mike, I just can't resist her."

"You got it bad, son."

"It was cool at first. Like I said, we would just hang out, talk shit, have a good time. We weren't even fuckin' then," Bobby said passionately as he drove. "But that night when I picked her up from Cynt's, we stopped at a couple of places, had some drinks on the way down to pick up the keys, so we were both kinda drunk. So, I'm drivin', and she says, 'You gonna give me some of that dick, nigga.' And I laughed at her and said 'No, I'm not.' She said, 'Yeah, you gonna finish what you started,' and she reaches over and starts pullin' down my zipper."

Mike started to laugh.

"I'm tryin' to drive and fight her off at the same time, but she gets it out anyway. Mike."

"What?"

"Mike."

"What?" Mike asked again, laughing.

"She sucked my dick all the way down the FDR Drive," Bobby said as he pulled in front of Cityscape.

When Mike and Bobby got out of the car, Mike saw Freeze's truck parked in front of the club. As they walked toward the club, Mike's thoughts drifted to Shy. He thought about Rio and what a good time they had there. He also remembered that was the first time Cassandra mentioned that she wanted to come back to New York to face her charges. Mike didn't want to think about that right now.

While they sat in the Cityscape and looked around for Sal Terrico, Bobby, Nick and Freeze enjoyed themselves with the ladies. Mike sat with them, watching, but it was obvious that his mind was someplace else. As the music pounded, Mike was taken back to Rio and their club-hopping nights. They didn't have to go far from their hotel to reach the clubs. In Copacabana, there were different parties every night. In Ipanema, they hit Baronetti, Nova

PAYBACK

Lounge and Spazio; Melt, in Leblon; and Sky Lounge in Lagoa.

When they returned to their room in the early hours of the morning, Mike and Shy were playfully drunk. Shy came into the room and plopped down on the first piece of furniture she got to. Mike laughed as he fumbled for the light switch without success.

"Never mind, baby. I'll just light a candle. It will be more romantic," Shy said as she fumbled for the matches. Once the candle was lit, it illuminated the room. "That's better."

Mike sat down next to her and Shy stood up. "Unzip me, please."

"Why did you wait until I sat down to ask me that?"

"Stop being so lazy." Shy laughed as Mike struggled to his feet. Mike took a step toward Shy and she turned around. He zipped down her dress and it fell to the floor to reveal her red lace bra and matching panties.

"Thank you," Shy said as Mike paused to admire her beauty. In his eyes, Shy was still the most beautiful woman he'd ever met. Shy kissed him on the cheek and started to walk toward the bathroom.

Mike grabbed her hand. "Come here," he said and pulled Shy into his arms. He kissed her lips and Shy began to unbutton Mike's shirt while he kissed her. Shy slid his shirt slowly off his shoulders and threw it to the floor. She ran her hands across his chest.

"I love you so much."

"I love you too," he said and unhooked her bra, kissed her lips and then her neck. Shy moaned as he slid her panties off. Shy stood naked in front of Mike, and Mike pulled her closer and kissed her on the lips as Shy helped him out of his pants. Once they were both naked, Shy gently pushed Mike away and walked out on the balcony. Naturally, Mike followed her.

They were in one of the penthouse suites, so neither was too worried about being seen. Mike walked up behind Shy and wrapped his arms around her. He ran his hands over her stomach. Shy spread her legs a little and Mike eased one finger between her legs and massaged her clit.

"Bend over and grab your ankles," Mike said as he ran his hands over her ass and then up and down her back.

"I'm too drunk to grab my ankles," Shy said as she held the rail. Mike knelt down and kissed her legs then stood slid his entire length inside of her, moving in and out slowly. Mike held on tightly and Shy bucked her hips wildly. Sweat dripped from their bodies as they made love with a spectacular view in front of them. Their bodies pounded into each other in fluid motion until she was about to cum. Then Mike suddenly stopped.

"What the fuck are you doing?"

"Come with me," Mike said and led Shy into the bedroom.

Shy lay down on the bed and Mike lay next to her. Shy's breasts seemed to glisten and her nipples grew harder as Mike ran his tongue across them. Shy got up on her knees and started kissing his chest, his stomach and finally his manhood. She stroked it, kissed it, ran her tongue along the length of it before easing it into her mouth. Shy opened her mouth wider and began to suck his manhood. Mike gently grabbed her head and began moving it slowly up and down until his length disappeared inside her.

They looked in each other's eyes. Mike reached for her face and pulled her toward him. Their tongues became entangled in passion. Mike kissed his way down to her body, lingering at the nipples. He slid his tongue inside her and moved it in and out slowly and gently. Mike spread her lips and tongued her clit. Shy grabbed his head and held it in place. Shy screamed in ecstasy.

"Black!" Nick yelled to him over the music, but Mike didn't seem to hear him. He was still lost in thoughts of Shy. "Black!"

"Huh?"

"You all right, man?"

"I'm good, Nick. Just thinkin'."

"I understand. You got a lot on your mind. We haven't seen Terrico in here yet, but we're in the right place, 'cause all of the dancers seem to know him. When he's here, he throws around a lot of money, so all the dancers love him. He's got one that's his favorite. Her name is Jaylyn, but she didn't come in tonight."

"That's probably the chick that was with him at Dirty Red's tonight."

"Could be," Nick said.

Mike looked around the club. "Where's Bobby?"

"He said that he needed some air and went outside."

Mike nodded, figuring that Bobby was outside on the phone, talking to either Pam or Cat or both. "So, what's up with your girl? She all right?"

"Yeah. I just wanted to make sure that she was gonna be safe after what Sally Fitz told me tonight."

"What did he have to say?" Mike asked, and Nick told him about the papers that the information broker, Paris, was killed over.

"I think that those papers give a detailed account of what we were doin' in South America. Before Freeze killed him, Felix said that there were stories in Washington about a drug eradication effort, and if those stories ever made their way to Capital Hill, there would be hell to pay. Sally Fitz said those papers are still in the open and the buyer is still looking for them, so I thought it was a good idea that I move Monika to a safer location."

"Who's the buyer?" Mike asked.

"I think its Diego, 'cause it was the General who was brokering the deal."

"Fuckin' Diego. You think that's what this shit is all about, these fuckin' papers?"

"I think so. If those papers surface and I get subpoenaed to testify, it could blow up a lot of people's shit. He killed Jett over that information and tried to kill me and Monika."

"But I hear you're hard to kill, Nick."

Chapter Fifteen

Even though she knew she had business in the morning, it had been another sleepless night for Jackie Washington. Not that sleepless nights were anything new to her. She had stayed up many a night playing poker, but this was something else entirely. She had been in bed for hours, but she couldn't make her mind shut down to allow her to rest. So, she thought about it.

She had killed somebody.

Looked him in the eye, and killed him.

Jackie had never even fired her guns before that night, much less killed anybody, and it bothered her. Truth was, it was eating her alive from the inside out.

Jackie could see the whole thing happening. *It plays like a movie,* Jackie thought. She could see herself walking through it each time she closed her eyes.

I need you to watch my back, she could hear Freeze say, *You armed?* Jackie could see herself unbuttoning her jacket and opening both sides to reveal a 9-

millimeter in each holster. *Always armed and extremely dangerous.* She could see herself walking behind Freeze until he saw Cynt coming toward him. Jackie couldn't hear what they said, but she could see Cynt pointing and Freeze moving quickly in that direction. It wasn't until she saw Freeze take his gun out that Jackie realized what was going on. That's where it all began to happen so fast. She didn't remember pulling her gun or Freeze grabbing the bottle, *Hey, muthafucka!* and Freeze smashing the bottle into the guy's face. She remembered thinking, *Damn, that shit musta hurt.* Then, *Freeze! Look out!* she could hear herself yelling and firing two shots. She couldn't remember anything after that except Travis taking the gun out of her hand and saying, *Don't worry, Jackie. You did what you had to do.*

It was so easy when she, Travis and Ronnie started out and hit their first spot. It was a jewelry store. Travis and Ronnie came through the door with guns drawn. Everybody down, Ronnie jumped the counter, grabbed the loot, and they were out. All Jackie did was drive the car. *Easy.*

After Freeze took his taste, they came away with $48,000. When Travis handed her $16,000 she was hooked. Sixteen thousand dollars just to drive a car, something she loved doing anyway, *Shit! This is it!* Who knew that money would lead her here? She had killed somebody, and Ronnie was dead.

Ronnie, Jackie thought. It was only now that she understood where Ronnie's head was after he shot that armored truck driver. *But what else could I do?*

That was the question she continued to ask herself. If she hadn't shot the man, Freeze would be dead. Then either she or Travis would've killed him anyway or been killed in the gunfight that would follow. She did the right thing, the only thing that she could do in those circumstances. But it was still the wrong thing. She never was overly religious, but she believed in God. She'd been taught the Ten Commandments in Sunday school. Thou shall not kill—*or was it thou shall not murder?* She wasn't sure, so she spent hours at her computer, researching the Commandments.

She found two versions of the Ten Commandments given in the Bible, the first in Exodus 20, and the second in Deuteronomy 5. It appeared that the preferred use was the version in Exodus. It was in Wikipedia, a free encyclopedia she found online that Jackie found the actual translation: "You shall not murder." It was there that she found that the Hebrew Bible makes a distinction between murdering and killing, and explicitly notes that murder is always a heinous sin, while killing is sometimes necessary, and in some cases, just in the eyes of God. Jackie thought that somehow she had found absolution for her crime at this Web site, and tried to get some much-needed sleep.

Jackie rolled over in bed, closer to Travis. They had been sleeping together since the night Ronnie was killed. Neither one of them wanted to be alone, and each needed the other's support. Eventually, they began having sex, and eventually, Jackie began to invite her old playmates home to play.

She looked over at the woman lying on the other side of Travis. Her name was Vonda, and she had become their playmate of choice. She was drop dead gorgeous, had a body that was to die for, and her sexual skills were extraordinary. Jackie first met her at Cynt's. Vonda was there with a guy who was boring her to tears. He had brought her there as a showpiece, a good luck charm, if you would, while he played poker. While she stood behind him looking distracted and ready to go, Jackie couldn't take her eyes off this red-bone brick house. She was just that damn fine.

Vonda was five feet eleven inches tall and weighed 150 pounds, with pretty brown eyes and curly hair that hung down the middle of her back. When the guy sent her to the bar to get him a drink, Jackie cashed herself out of the game and went after her. Jackie gave Vonda her cell number, and eventually they hooked up for drinks. Jackie seduced her that same night.

It wasn't too long after that that Jackie introduced Vonda to Travis. He didn't seem to mind. In fact, he was enjoying it. He commented once that they should have been doing this all along. At first, it was a way to keep his mind off Me'shelle, the woman he loved. Travis missed Me'shelle. Even though he felt that she had used him to get what she wanted and let him go, he still believed that on some level Me'shelle still loved him too.

As for Jackie, she was willing to go along with part of that—the part about Me'shelle using Travis and dumping him. "But, Travis, if she really loved you, she wouldn't do you the way she did," Jackie told him. "The bitch just foul, and that's all there is to it."

She had considered having Me'shelle killed. Even went as far as to ask Freeze to do it, but he told her that she needed to get over it. After that, she thought about doing it herself. *I could walk right up on that bitch and blow her brains out.*

But that was then. Now Jackie knew that she was no killer. She was a chemist, and a damn good one. That life seemed far away now too. Right now, she was a part-time gambler, part-time robber with a job to run in a couple of hours.

It would be Vonda's first time doing a job with Travis and Jackie. They were going to hit a jewelry store. Vonda would hit the display cases while Travis forced the manager to open the safe. This would be Jackie's first time calling the job, which meant that she was responsible for the safety and security of the team. It was a position that she lobbied Travis long and hard for. Now Jackie wondered if she was up to the challenge. But in her heart, she knew that when the time came, she would do her job.

Chapter Sixteen

Detectives Kirkland and Richards arrived in the briefing room for their assignment with the DEA.

"Gentlemen, this is Detectives Kirkland and Richards. They are on loan to us from the NYPD homicide division." Once Agent DeFrancisco introduced them to the agents involved in the operation, he turned things over to the agent in charge, Pete Vinnelli, who started the briefing.

"All right, gentlemen, settle down and let's get to business. Our objective is Mike Black. We have information that he is a major player in the drug traffic in this city, and has been for years." Detective Kirkland immediately raised his hand. "Detective?" agent Vinnelli said.

"Can you share the source of that information?"

"Oh, agent DeFrancisco failed to mention that the detective has been investigating Mr. Black for years and doesn't believe that Mr. Black has any involvement in drug traffic. He thinks we're wasting our time here," agent Vinnelli said, not hiding his

PAYBACK

contempt for Kirk and his involvement in this operation. The other agents looked at Kirk, and the grumbles began.

"Settle down, gentlemen. I'm sure that despite his personal opinion about the objective, the detective will give us one hundred percent. Besides, I think that his involvement will give this operation a certain objectivity, as I'm sure the detective will be quite vocal if anything we do doesn't pass the sniff test. And I want this operation run by the book. Are we all clear on this? That means no shortcuts, no slip-ups. I don't want this asshole to wiggle out of this because we fucked up," Vinnelli said to everyone before turning his attention back to Kirk.

"Now, to answer your question, detective, no, I can't share the source of the information. What I can tell you is that a meeting was held in a club in the Bahamas yesterday. That meeting was between a couple of middlemen from a Peruvian drug cartel and DEA agent Roman Patterson. The meeting was held at a club called Black's Paradise, and it is owned, as the name indicates, by Mike Black."

"Was Black present at this meeting?" Kirk asked.

"No, but his wife, Cassandra Black, a.k.a. Cassandra Sims, a.k.a. Shy was present at the meeting. At that meeting, agent Patterson was murdered, along with one of the middlemen that Patterson was able to kill before he was murdered. Now, your job here, detective, is to detail for us everything you know about him and his operation. Where he does business and who he does it with. And I wanna know right here, right now, if we can count on you, detective."

"You got something you're tryin' to say to me, agent Vinnelli?"

"My office, detective."

Kirk got up and followed Vinnelli to the door. Richards got up too. "Where are you goin'?"

"He's my partner. You got something to say, you say it to both of us," Richards said defiantly.

Vinnelli took a deep breath and opened the door to the briefing room. "By all means, detective. Why don't you join us." Kirk and Richards walked out of the briefing room and Vinnelli followed them out, slamming the door behind him. He led them across the hall to his office and slammed that door as well.

Vinnelli stood face to face with Kirk. "I'm gonna lay it on the line for you, detective. I don't want you here. I believe your presence here compromises the success of this operation."

"And why is that, agent Vinnelli?"

"You've been investigating this asshole for drug-related murder after drug-related murder for years, and you've never made a case, never even arrested him. Why is that, detective?"

Kirk stepped to Vinnelli's chest. "What are you trying to say?"

"I'm not trying to say anything, detective. I already said what I have to say."

"Fair enough. Now, let me tell you something. I'm gonna do my job, agent Vinnelli. And if it turns out that Black is involved in drug trafficking, I wanna be the one to put the cuffs on him." Kirk started to walk away, but turned around quickly. "And if you ever call me out again, I'll kick your fuckin' ass."

"Fair enough."

PAYBACK

"Glad we understand each other," Kirk said and walked out of the office, followed closely by Richards and Vinnelli.

The three men returned to the room, and Vinnelli continued his briefing. Then Vinnelli turned the briefing over to Detective Kirkland, who broke down in more detail than anyone on the team was prepared for, everything he knew about Mike Black.

Chapter Seventeen

Melinda Brown woke up early that morning and rolled out of bed. Still naked, she walked to the window and cracked the drapes. She was twenty-eight years old, the youngest of four beautiful girls. Melinda was tall and fine. Her hair was cut short, oval-shaped eyes, high cheekbones, full lips, and her skin was light brown. Each of her sisters had her first child before turning sixteen. Melinda knew that wasn't the life for her.

Very early in life, Melinda learned to parlay her looks into getting everything she ever wanted, and for a time, she had it all. Melinda was living the good life. She drove a 500 Benz; she still had the car, actually. Melinda lived in condo with a view of the Long Island Sound for which she paid no rent. She shopped in all the fashionable places that New York had to offer, and ate in the best restaurants. She went to Broadway shows and traveled the Caribbean. There was even talk of a trip to Europe. She missed going to fights in Las Vegas and Atlantic City. She even missed almost freezing to death watching those damn Jets games at the Meadowlands. Most of all, she missed being Mike Black's woman.

Melinda had been introduced to Black by Freeze at a strip club. Melinda was trying to get a job as a dancer, but she just didn't have the patience to deal with the clientele. Melinda and Black were going along just fine, until that bitch Shy came along. Then everything changed. Black used to say one of the things he liked most about Melinda was that she was no trouble at all. But that was then.

After Black dropped her for Shy, Melinda was alone. She went back to her condo and packed her things and waited for somebody to tell her that she had to move, but no one ever did, and no bills ever came. She assumed that the condo was paid for and when the bills came, they were just paid automatically by whoever handled that menial task for Black.

Once Melinda got over the initial shock of her new situation, she began to think about what she was going to do next. She had always been a gangster's girl and had become accustomed to a certain lifestyle. Melinda saw no reason to change that. Why should she?

She quickly gravitated to the first gangster she found. That was Derrick Washington. But it wasn't the same. At the time, he was Chilly's top lieutenant. Now, with Chilly dead, D-Train had risen to power. It was his time now. Now he was moving against Freeze.

Melinda looked over at D-Train as he moved around in bed. She didn't have a lot of respect for Curl, a nickname people called him behind his back. The name was a holdover from the old days, when he wore a very bad Jheri-curl long after it went out of style. D-Train had built his rep on being ruthless, but to Melinda, he was weak and easily controlled. And stupid. *My God, that is one stupid nigga.* How could she respect a man so stupid he allowed her to tell him what to do? The answer was simple; she couldn't. *At least he got a big dick,* Melinda thought as she looked at him. She shook her head and longed for the days when she had a man. Melinda was still in love with Mike Black.

"You're up early, baby," D-Train said from the bed. "You a'ight?"

"I'm fine," Melinda said as she returned to the bed. She slid between the sheets and reached for his manhood. "What's wrong with you?" Melinda asked when it didn't respond immediately to her touch.

"Nothing, baby. I just got a lot on my mind, that's all."

"Like what?" Melinda asked as she continued to stroke him.

"Five of my people are dead, baby. All killed by Freeze. I gotta do something."

"They're dead 'cause you aren't listening to me, or your thugs are too stupid to follow instructions," Melinda told him, still stroking him until he was hard.

"What you talkin' bout? You the one who said to post up in their spots."

"See, that's what I'm talkin' 'bout. You aren't listening to me." Melinda straddled his torso and slid her body down on him. "That feels good," she said and began moving up and down on him slowly. "What I told you to do was send a couple of people into their spots. Check things out, see how things are run, make some friends, build alliances. That's what I told you to do. Not go in there and try to set up shop."

D-Train said nothing. He lay on his back and enjoyed what Melinda was making him feel.

"But that's what they did; ran up in there and started slingin'. The only thing that could happen was for somebody to call Freeze, and what did you expect him to do?"

Again, D-Train didn't answer. He was in ecstasy, watching her, feeling her. And besides, she was right.

"Exactly what he did, he killed them. That's what he does, but that's all he's good for, killin'. Freeze ain't that bright, baby, and you can take him out, but you have to take your time. I know how they run things. I know how to take him, but you got to do exactly what I say."

"Okay, okay, brain. What you think I should do?"

"You're right about one thing: You gotta bust back or Birdie and his people will think that you're weak."

D-Train thought for a second. Birdie was his rival for power. If Birdie saw him as weak, he and his people would go off on their own, and that would be bad for business. "I should call Freeze and—"

"No, silly. That's the last thing you want to do. I know your ego wants to sit down with Freeze, but that is not the way. What you gotta do is make people see Freeze for the stupid, weak muthafucka that he is."

"I'm listening," D-Train said.

"You're gonna have to change your tactics. Don't send any more people into their spots. That's over. They'll be waitin' for you now. What you need to do now is hit them. Take their money. You rob them, let people know that Freeze ain't—" Melinda paused. She started to say "Freeze ain't Mike Black," but she knew better. D-Train hated for Melinda to even mention that name. *Last time I said Mike Black, his dick went soft.*

"Let people know that Freeze ain't the man. That they can be touched. Make Freeze come to you. That puts you in a position of strength."

"Yeah, I'll hit one of their spots," D-Train said and tried to push himself deeper inside Melinda.

"What did I just say?" Melinda asked and moaned her approval. She ground her hips harder into him. "That's over. They'll be waitin' for you now."

"Where should we hit?" D-Train asked, breathing heavily.

"Impressions."

"Bobby's club? You out your fuckin' mind. That's fuckin' suicide. They got so much security up in that bitch it ain't even fuckin' funny. On top of that, they always got at least three, four off-duty cops working outside, usually more. How we gonna get past them?"

"Do I have to think of everything?"

D-Train gave her a look that screamed *YES!*

"You have two people, a man and a woman, start an argument in the parking lot away from the cops, but not too far that the cops can't hear them. The cops will think it's a domestic dispute, and at least one of them will come over there to see what's goin' on. When they see the cops coming, have the woman fire a gun. All the cops will run toward the shot."

"I see, create a diversion."

Melinda rolled her eyes. D-Train pumped harder. "Once the cops are away from the front door, send in four men; one to watch the cops from the door, one to cover the hall leading to the club, one covers security while the other one gets the money. It doesn't matter how much money they get. The fact that you hit Bobby's spot will be enough to bring Freeze to the table."

"Yes!" D-Train screamed.

"He'll be callin' you beggin' for a meeting. And at that meeting, you'll kill him."

"Yes!"

Chapter Eighteen

Bobby pulled up in front of Mike's house and put his car in park. He was tired, hadn't gotten much sleep the night before. Even though it was early in the morning when he dropped Mike off, Bobby didn't go home. He went by Cat's apartment and did what they do. "Had the best sex I ever had," Bobby said as he got out of the car and went to ring the bell.

From inside the house, Mike could see Bobby coming, and opened the door. "Come on in and sit down," Mike said then took a closer look at Bobby. "You look like shit."

Bobby walked straight to the bar and poured himself a drink. "Thank you, Mike. You're lookin' very good yourself. But shit would be a step up from the way I feel," he said as he turned up his drink and poured another one.

"What's wrong with you?"

"Didn't get much sleep last night."

"Why not? You and Pam up all night?"

PAYBACK

"No." Bobby paused. "I didn't get home until after nine."

Mike laughed. "Shit, Bobby, is the pussy all that?"

Bobby just looked at Mike and shook his head. "When I got home, Pam was sitting in her spot, waiting for me. First thing out her mouth was, 'Where the fuck you been?' I told her that I was out lookin' for Shy with you. She looked at me and said, 'That's your story. You were with Mike lookin' for Shy, right? That's your story.' "

Bobby recounted the story for Mike.

"Yeah, that's where I been," Bobby said and started toward stairs.

Pam got up immediately and followed him up the steps. "You look tired, baby."

"Yeah, I'll nod for a couple of hours then I'll go pick up Mike and we'll get back to it," he said and went in their bedroom with Pam on his heels.

"You didn't get any sleep, huh?"

"No, I told you we been riding all night."

"Just you and Mike, huh? Ridin' all night, huh? Just like the old days, huh?"

"What the fuck is wrong with you?"

Pam gave Bobby a wide-eyed look. "Oh, you wanna know what the fuck is wrong with me? Is that what you wanna know?"

"Yes, Pam. What the fuck is wrong with you?"

"Where were you last night and this morning, Bobby?"

"I told you—"

"And don't tell me that you were with Mike."

"Pam, I was with Mike. Shy's been kidnapped, and we been out all night looking for her."

"Did you find her?"

"No! I told you I wanna grab a couple of hours sleep and hit the streets again."

"Bobby," Pam said. "I'ma ask you this one more time, and this time I want the truth. And don't give me that shit about you being out with Mike all night, 'cause I know you weren't with him, at least not all night."

"This is insane, Pam. Why don't you call Mike and ask him?"

"Why? So he can lie to me too?"

"Fuck this," Bobby said and started for the door.

Pam moved quickly to block the door before Bobby got to it. "Who is she, Bobby? Who is the woman who called our house?"

"I don't know what you're talkin' about, Pam. What woman?"

"At six-thirty this morning, some woman called here and said I don't have to worry about where you are 'cause you were safe there with her."

"I have no idea who that could have been. I was with Mike." Bobby lied to his wife, but now he was thinking, *Goddamn it, I'ma kill Cat.*

"Well, she must have been with Mike too, because she called from your phone!" Pam yelled.

At that point, Bobby looked down at the cell phone on his hip and knew that he couldn't say he'd lost it. He was caught.

"It was just that simple, Mike. She had me."

"How'd she get your phone?" Mike asked.

"I was asleep."

PAYBACK

"She took your phone while you were sleeping and called Pam." Mike laughed. "Do we need to roll by her spot so I can kill her?"

"You know you don't kill women, Mike." Bobby laughed right along with him.

"You're right. I'll send Freeze over there right now," Mike said, laughing, and then he got real serious. "No, no, wait a minute. I got a better idea. I'll send Wanda instead," Mike said and busted out laughing again. "Hold up. I know Freeze had to know about you and this Cat woman."

"I told Freeze not to tell you."

"Why'd you tell him that?" Mike asked, wondering why Freeze had chosen to tell him about it now.

"You didn't need to know."

"I guess I didn't. But don't you think you need to put a stop to this?"

"This isn't the first time she called Pam."

"What?"

"First time she did it, I had just called Pam and told her I would be home in a couple of hours. She asks if she could use my phone, I hand it to her, she says, 'Never mind.' But what she does is redial the number and put the phone down. And starts talking to me."

"Damn, Bobby."

"Only thing that saved me then was we must have been ridin' through a dead zone because the call dropped."

"Now I know you need to put a stop to this . . . unless you plannin' to leave Pam."

"You're crazy as she is if you think that I'm gonna leave my family," Bobby said definitely.

"Is she?"

120

"Is she what?"

"Is she crazy?"

"As hell. And strong as hell."

"I heard that about crazy people. I heard crazy women got the best pussy. I guess that must be true too, huh, Bobby," Mike said, still laughing. "How you know how strong she is?"

"I had to fight her off this morning to get out of the house."

"You're kiddin'."

"No! I told you that I fell asleep, right? So when I woke up, she's lying next to me, sleeping."

"This must have been after she called Pam."

"You gonna let me tell the story, or you wanna ask stupid questions that you already know the answer to?"

"Both."

"Yeah, this was after she called Pam. Happy now?"

"Very. You gonna finish the story or what?"

"Anyway, I wake up and get dressed, but she wakes up before I can get outta there. She says, 'Where you think your goin'?' I told her that I was goin' home and I would get with her later if I had some time. She jumps out of bed naked, talking about I can't leave, how she's tired of me fuckin' her and leavin' her. That she love me and Pam couldn't possibly love me like she love me, and all Pam got over her is the kids and shit, so I need to get back in bed and give her some more dick so she can start having my babies. I said, 'Your ass is crazy' and started to leave, but she ran to the door and tried to block it. I said 'Stop fuckin' around, Cat. I gotta go.' She's like, 'No! You gotta fuck me before you go.' So I tried to move her out of the

121

way, but she starts wrestling with me. I had to end up picking her up and carrying her out of the way. Then I tried to leave again, but by the time I get out in the hallway, she jumped on my back. So, I shake her off my back, and she falls on the floor hard, but she gets right up and starts wrestling with me again. So, here I am, at eight in the morning, wrestling with a naked woman in the hallway."

"How'd you get out of there? You didn't hurt her, did you?"

"No, I didn't kick her ass, but I started to. I ended up picking her naked ass up and carrying her back in her apartment, threw her on the bed and got the fuck outta there."

Mike laughed at him. Again.

"This shit ain't funny," Bobby said, laughing right along with Mike.

"Yes it is, Bobby. This whole shit is funny as hell. I just can't see you at six-four, wrestling in the hall with a naked woman. That shit is too funny."

"Yeah, it would be funny if it was happening to somebody else."

"You need to shut that bitch down, Bobby. Getting pussy is one thing, but when she starts calling Pam, it's time to shut the bitch down. Unless you planning on leaving Pam for this crazy muthafucka."

"I told you I ain't leaving my family. I love Pam."

"Then what you gonna do?"

"I don't know. But I gotta do something."

Chapter Nineteen

"It just doesn't make any sense, Pat," Kirk said to his partner.

"What doesn't?" Richards asked

"Black having a meeting with drug dealers in his own place. Black is smarter than that."

"Maybe he didn't know about it. I mean, he wasn't there. Maybe she set the whole thing up."

"But Simmons is there ridin' shotgun over her drug meeting, and Black doesn't know about it? Give me a fuckin' break."

"They only said they had reason to believe that Simmons was there."

"This shit is weak, Pat. He was there. That picture they have of him was taken recently."

"What makes you so sure?" Richards asked.

"You saw that picture, Pat. Didn't he have that same scar under his eye last week when we saw him?"

Richards thought about it. "He damn sure did."

PAYBACK

"He was there; they know he was there. I got a feeling that things didn't happen down there the way they say it did."

"Why don't you just call Simmons and ask him?"

Kirk looked at Richards like he was stupid, but then he thought about it. "That's not a bad idea. But what do you say we just drop by his place."

When Nick opened the door, he looked a little groggy. He had stayed a little too long at Cityscape the night before, had one too many lap dances and way too many shots of Johnnie Black. "Kirk?" *What the fuck does he want?* Nick thought. He didn't have time for Kirk now. He had to leave soon if he wanted to catch Freddie, an old contact of his.

"Yeah, Kirk. Mind if we come in?"

"Come on in, gentlemen. I always have time to talk to New York's finest," Nick said and stepped aside.

Once the detectives were inside, Kirk asked, "Going somewhere?"

"As a matter of fact, I was."

"We need to ask you some questions, Simmons."

"What do you wanna know?"

"You seen Black lately?" Kirk asked nonchalantly.

"Saw him last night. This morning, actually."

"When did he get in?"

"Yesterday."

Just like that slime Marshall said, Kirk thought. "He up here on business?"

Nick looked at Kirk and then to Richards. There was a point to all these questions, and he was willing to go along to see where Kirk was going with this. But not for long. "He's got some business to take care of."

"What kind of business?"

"Let's stop dancing around, Kirk. What do you wanna know?"

"We have information that you and Black met with a couple of drug middlemen at Black's club in the Bahamas a couple of days ago. So, I'll ask you again. What kind of business is he up here doing?"

"First of all, let's get one thing straight. Me and Black weren't involved in any meeting with anybody in his club."

"So, you weren't in the Bahamas at Black's club?"

"Yeah, I was there, but Black wasn't there."

"Who you meet with then, Nick?" Richards asked sarcastically.

"I didn't meet with anybody, Pat," Nick responded in kind. "I had drinks with Black's wife."

"Shy," Richards said. "You had drinks with Shy."

"Who?"

"Cassandra Sims, a.k.a. Shy," Richards taunted. "A.k.a. Cassandra Black. Mike Black's wife."

"Look, Simmons," Kirk interrupted, "we know what happened in that club. We know you and Shy met with two drug middlemen. What's going on, Nick? Black gettin' back in the game? He up here to set things in motion?"

Nick thought for a moment before answering. *Kirk gets around, knows people, hears things. He might be some help with this,* he thought, but Kirk was a cop, a good cop, so he decided to proceed with caution. "His wife was kidnapped. That's what Black is doin' here."

"By who?" Richards demanded to know.

"You ever hear of a guy named Sal Terrico? Runs with some South Americans. They're the middlemen you keep askin' about. Check with the DEA. They might have an ongoin' operation involving him."

"Slow down, Simmons. You say this Terrico guy that kidnapped Black's wife is involved with the DEA?"

"No, what I said was Terrico is one of the middlemen, and that the DEA might have an ongoing operation involving him," Nick replied, treading carefully.

"So, what does the DEA have to do with Terrico?"

"They're probably looking at him in connection with the murder of an agent named Roman Patterson."

At that point, Kirk was sure that something wasn't right. The DEA never mentioned anything about Terrico being involved with the agent's murder. They made it seem like Black was involved. *But why?* "I need you to tell me everything you know about this."

"Why, Kirk? Why should I tell you?"

"'Cause I know some things; things you need to know."

"All right, Kirk," Nick said. "Agent Patterson was at Black's club in the Bahamas. He was meeting with Terrico and two other men. Both of them were Latinos, probably South American. During that meeting, one of the Latinos shot and killed Patterson. There was some shooting. During that shooting, one of the Latinos was killed, Terrico and the other guy got away with Shy."

"I thought she was a part of the meeting. Why'd they take her?"

"She wasn't involved in their meeting. They used her as a hostage to get out of there."

Chapter Twenty

"You just got to trust me, Simmons."

It wasn't easy, but Kirk finally got out of Nick's apartment, and more importantly, got out of the apartment without giving him any information. *What now?* Kirk knew something wasn't right with all this. *Why the different stories? Why was the team led to believe that Mike Black had something to do with agent Patterson's death? If Black isn't involved, why is the DEA investigating him?* Those were all good questions, none of which he had the answers to. Whatever was going on, there was one thing he was sure of: He needed to cover his ass and do it quick.

The first step was to make a call. "Captain, this is Kirk. Listen, there is something weird going on here that I need to make you aware of." He went on to tell his captain about the inconsistencies in the stories about what went on two days ago at Black's Paradise.

"Wait a minute, Kirk. If she wasn't involved in the meeting, and one of the Latinos Patterson was meeting with shot him, what the fuck are they investigating Black for?"

"That's exactly my point," Kirk said as Detective Richards came into his office. He motioned for Richards to sit down and be quiet.

"And if there is some shit in this, that means that asshole Marshall is in it with the fuckin' DEA. Fuckin' state senator, shit!"

"This could get messy."

"Tell me about it."

"Look, Captain, I checked with Narcotics like you told me to, and they agree with me. Black's got no share in the drug game."

"I know. I talked to Sanchez too. So, if that's the case, they're either after Black for some other reason and they're using drugs as a cover, or they're using him to divert attention from the real players."

"Or both," Kirk threw in.

"In either case, it's political. Thanks for the heads up, Kirk," the captain said.

He was about to hang up when Kirk yelled, "Slow down, captain. Whatever you're about to do, I need to be a part of," he said quickly. "What are you about to do?"

"First thing to do is find out exactly what went on down there. Hold on, Kirk." While the captain called the Bahamian police, Kirk explained the situation to his partner. When the captain came back on the line, he told Kirk, "The Bahamian police confirmed your guy's version."

"What do we do now?" Kirk asked.

"I'm gonna start covering our asses and maybe, just maybe, take down a bad guy or two. You do nothing. Hear me, Kirk?" the captain ordered. "Nothing unless I authorize it."

"Yes, sir," Kirk said quietly.

Chapter Twenty-one

His name was Paul Clay, and this would be the day that he stepped up. This would be the day that he introduced himself to the big time. He'd made up his mind, after today there would be no more small-time anything for him. Today was the day that he would become a real player in this game.

The truth of the matter was that Clark Kent, that's what they called him, was small-time; small-time drug dealer, small-time robber, small-time pimp, small-time hustler.

They called him Clark Kent because of the thick, black-framed glasses he wore. He didn't care about the name. Those glasses had earned him names like nerd and schoolboy. While he was in jail for armed robbery, he was Brother Malcolm. Paul actually liked being called Clark Kent. In a strange way, it made him feel powerful. It made him feel like he was Superman and only he knew it.

This would be the day that Paul made a name for himself. See, if he was to improve his position, now was the perfect time. With Chilly dead, what was left of his crew had splintered into two factions, one loyal to D-Train, and the other loyal to Birdie.

For the time being, D-Train had grabbed power and was trying to prove he was worthy by moving on Freeze and the so-called dead zone. If that move was unsuccessful, then Birdie would surely step up his game and try to force D-Train out and into an early grave. But if Train was successful in eliminating Freeze, then he would surely crush Birdie, unite the factions, and everybody could go back to making money. Paul was there to make sure that happened. His plan was simple. He would be the man that killed Freeze.

Clark Kent sat patiently outside Cross County Mall in Yonkers, because he knew that she would be there. He had spent hours the night before on the phone with her, and she promised that she would be shopping at the mall that next afternoon.

She went to great lengths to make sure that he understood that she was a woman who was used to being taken care of, and used to a certain style, a style that he couldn't afford. "Baby, you know I love you, right? We can hang out and kick it or whatever, and you can get this pussy, but until you start stackin' some serious paper, the kind of paper where you drop ten grand on me 'cause it's a sunny day, I will never be yours," she told him on more than one occasion, and it was unacceptable. He had to have her. Clark Kent was in love. He was in love with Pauleen. There was only one problem with him loving Pauleen. She was Freeze's woman.

PAYBACK

Shortly after Clark Kent got out of jail, he met Pauleen. She was coming out of Macy's on 34th Street. He gave her his number and she called him once in a while because she thought he was cute. But as hard as he tried, she would never see him. Pauleen told him that not only was she with Freeze, but she had a man on the side that took good care of her. This went on for a year before she finally agreed to see him.

Pauleen was worth the wait. Clark Kent was hooked the first time she set it out for him. *Now I understand why they call her good pussy Pauleen.* When he asked about her man on the side, you know, the one that was taking such good care of her, she said that she had grown tired of him and moved up to bigger and better sex with Clark Kent. What he heard was that Freeze had found out about it and killed the guy. It was a fate that he planned on avoiding, and it just gave him one more reason that he had to kill Freeze.

"I kill Freeze," Clark Kent said out loud while he sat in his 73 Nova, "D-Train will blast Birdie, set me up for killin' Freeze, and Pauleen will be all mine."

It wasn't too long after that when he saw Freeze's truck pull into a parking space. He watched nervously as Pauleen got out, and she and Freeze went into the mall. She was dressed in orange from head to toe. Everything matched: her outfit, her shoes, her accessories. She looked so good to him. It excited Clark Kent just to see her. He wanted to get out of his car and run to her, but that wasn't what he was there for.

The thing to do now was prepare. He had thought long and hard about how he would kill Freeze. His first thought was to walk right up on Freeze when he exited the mall with Pauleen. He would look her in the eye, make some comment about this being for her, and blow Freeze's brains out. *That's not strong enough.* He would walk up on Freeze and tell him that he was in love with Pauleen and she loved him, and for that reason, he had to die. *Yeah, that's it,* he thought. But then he reconsidered. Suppose Freeze wasn't tryin' to hear that shit and shot him before he got a chance to declare his love and kill Freeze. No, the thing to do was to wait on them to come out of the mall and roll by Freeze, blastin'.

He briefly gave some thought to the fact that if he did the drive-by thing, Pauleen wouldn't know that he was the man who killed Freeze. But he slowly came to the conclusion that it was best that way, just in case Pauleen wasn't happy about the fact he had shot her golden goose and decided to snitch.

So, he waited in the car for somebody to move out of a parking space that would give him the best angle of approach. There wasn't any rush. He knew how Pauleen shopped; they would be in there for hours.

Pauleen was starving by the time she and Freeze got to the mall, so the first thing she wanted to do was eat. She suggested that they grab something at Applebee's before they started shopping.

Freeze didn't care. He had other things on his mind. The night before had been a quiet night, which meant that he got no reports of any of D-Train's people setting up in any of their spots. Freeze doubted that it was over just like that. What he had to do now was figure out what D-Train had planned, and stop it before it started.

PAYBACK

His conversation with Black and Bobby about the situation kept rolling around in his mind. *He sees this as an opportunity. Me gone, Bobby layin' back. Makes it look like your strength is exhausted. We need to deal with this now or other muthafuckas will raise up outta nowhere to try some shit like this.* He had to wonder if maybe Black and Bobby thought that he was weak.

After they left Applebee's, Pauleen went to Baker's Shoes. After she looked at a few pairs of shoes, she settled on a pair of Mojo sandals, a thong-styled sandal with rhinestone detailing on the upper straps and 3-inch wedge heels. "What do you think, Freeze?"

"They look a'ight," Freeze replied without looking. *We need to start takin' it to them, Black. Just fall up in there and start blastin' like we used to.* Maybe that was the answer. Bring back the old days. Shoot first and never get to the ask questions part. He had always thought that they had become too soft lately, but it wasn't his fault. Even though he was running the day to day operations, it was Wanda who was calling the shots.

"But I like these too," Pauleen said, holding up a dressy sandal with a snake-and-leather upper, hooded ankle strap, and lacquered platform wedge heel by Wild Pair.

"Fuck it, get 'em both," Freeze told her, still thinking about the old days. In his opinion, Wanda was now too deeply involved in the business. Sure, Wanda had done a great job at making money for all of them, but back then, Black was very definite about what parts of the business he allowed her to become involved in. Wanda had no say at all about how Black and Bobby ran things. Now, Wanda had her hands up in every part of the business, and she was always on him about the way he chose to handle things. That had to stop.

Once they were finished in Baker's they passed a Com-Fit Shoes. Pauleen started to go in, but decided to go to Nine West first. There she found a gorgeous sling in a metallic dust kidskin and a pair of Enzo Angiolini's. Then it was on to Bath & Body Works. She wanted to pick up some True Blue Spa, All in a Clay's Work Detoxifying Facial Mask. "What's that for?" Freeze asked.

"It absorbs excess oil and draws impurities from the skin. I use it once a week."

"You don't need that shit," Freeze said as they walked to the register.

"Why not?"

"'Cause you ain't got no impurities in you skin. That shit is flawless."

"Yeah, that's because I use stuff like this to keep myself beautiful for you, baby," Pauleen said and gave Freeze a kiss on the cheek. Their next stop was CeBon Cosmetics, where it seemed like Pauleen tried every fragrance before settling on Issey Miyake for her and one for him. After that, Pauleen dragged Freeze into Charade Fashions, but she didn't see anything that she liked.

That wasn't the case in Wilson's Suede and Leather. Pauleen found an Italian leather belted briefcase. "Check this out," Pauleen told Freeze. "It has a phone case, and a detachable cosmetic bag with a mirror."

"Just get it and let's go," Freeze said and walked out of the store. He thought about what Black always said about understanding your enemy. *The thing to do now is figure out what your enemies are plannin' and stop them.* He thought about the way that D-Train was coming at him. That wasn't the way, sending people into the houses to set up, and each of them meeting the same fate. Maybe Black was right. The smart move was to defeat them without any fighting. He needed to out-think him, not out-fight him.

Maybe that's all Wanda was trying to do was to make me think.

Then they came to her favorite store, Victoria's Secret. Pauleen loved Victoria's Secret, and not just for the sexy lingerie, although she loved that too and had tons of it. It was because of the variety that they carried. She started with a Point d'esprit sequined babydoll. "Side slits, lace trim, adjustable straps, matching V-string. Sweet," Pauleen said and picked out a satin robe with a shawl collar and tie belt. But it didn't stop there. She found a lace-up mesh corseted Anna Paul silk floral babydoll. Next Pauleen tried on an Allen Schwartz crinkle chiffon cami, a lace racer back bra-top tank.

Then they moved on to Macy's.

"Baby, these are Blue London jeans. Top-stitched, ultra sexy jean in black platinum." Pauleen liked those, but they weren't going to work for every outfit. Then she found some DKNY jeans and a pair of Michael Kors Greenwich stretch jean, and a sexy strapless dress with allover soft pleats and sparkling bands of contrast sequins for added glamour. The short, flirty skirt hit at mid-thigh; side zip, of course, by Allen Schwartz.

On the way to the car, Pauleen wanted to stop at Nail City to get her nails and toes done. "Fuck that shit," Freeze said. "We been here too damn long already."

"Okay, okay," Pauleen said and struggled to the car with her bags. Freeze's hands were full of bags too, but he didn't mind. Even though he complained about it the whole time he was there, Freeze enjoyed shopping with Pauleen. It was one of the few chances that he afforded himself to treat his woman like a queen. *Besides, she was light today. All this cost only five grand.*

"I don't know what you need all that shit for anyway," Freeze said. "You're not gonna wear half of that shit."

"Well, if you would take me out sometimes instead of runnin' the streets all day and night, then maybe I would have someplace to go."

That's when Freeze saw a car pulling out of a space near where he was parked. Out of the corner of his eye, Freeze noticed the old Chevy Nova speed up and come right for them. As the speeding car approached, Freeze saw the gun. "Get down!" he yelled to Pauleen.

He dropped to the ground, reaching for his gun. Freeze fired back at the car as it sped away. He quickly got to his feet and chased after the car, firing shots as he ran. But it was too late. The car was too far away to hit, or even to see the license plate. All that Freeze could tell was the make and model.

"Chevy Nova, looks like a '73 model," Freeze said as he walked back to Pauleen. He noticed that a small crowd had formed around her. "Always got to be the center of attention," he said as he pushed through the crowd.

PAYBACK

Freeze stopped dead in his tracks and dropped to his knees. Pauleen lay on the ground, surrounded by her shopping bags, in a pool of her own blood. "Pauleen," Freeze whispered and took her hand in his, but she was already gone.

Chapter Twenty-two

Nick drove to the post office on White Plains Road and waited. He had been there for almost an hour when a late model dark blue Ford Crown Victoria pulled into the parking lot. A tall, slender white man got out and went inside. Nick got out of the car and waited for him to come out. As soon as he did, Nick walked up on him.

"Excuse me. Do you have change for a dollar?" Nick asked. The man turned around slowly. "Gotta make a phone call."

"I don't have any dimes," he replied.

"Two nickels will do."

"That's an old code, Nick. I was about to shoot you."

"I'm glad you didn't shoot me, Freddie. You still living dangerously?"

"Me? I should be asking you that. What are you doin' here?"

"I need some help."

139

PAYBACK

"Oh shit. I knew I was gonna regret not shooting you. What is it?"

"You ever hear of a guy named Paris and some papers he was trying to get his hands on?"

"Doesn't ring any bells, but meet me here same time tomorrow. I'll see what I can find out."

After Freddie left, Nick got back in his car and drove away to talk to Monika. When he took her out of the hospital, Nick didn't have time to explain what was going on. He just rushed her out of there and took her somewhere she'd be safe.

When he got to the safe hideout, Nick told Monika everything that had been going on, from the DEA agent being killed to Shy's kidnapping, to his conversation with Sally Fitz.

"Sally Fitz! That slimy bastard," Monika said. "He didn't give you the money he owes me?"

"No, sorry. He didn't even mention it."

"I didn't think so. Since he wasn't talkin' about payin' me the money he owes me, what's the slimy bastard talkin' about?"

"You remember a guy, called himself Paris?"

"Grey boy, thought he was cool, always used to wear sunglasses at night?"

"That's him."

"What about him?" Monika asked.

"I'm not gonna bore you with the Pam Grier story he told me, but one of his mules left a package in the open."

"And?"

"Sal didn't know who the buyer was, but General Peterson was brokering the deal."

"What was in the package?"

"He said it's got somethin' to do with South America and drugs."

"Stop right there, Nick. What are you tryin' to say?"

"That I think that package has something to do with us, and that the buyer is Diego Estabon."

"So you think it had something to do with what we were doin' down there?"

"I don't know for sure," Nick replied. "But I can't get past what Felix said."

"What's that?"

"That if what we were doin' down there became public knowledge, there'd be hell to pay in Washington. That's why they had to get rid of us."

"I think you're right. I mean, you said it yourself. There we were in South America, small teams, each working independently, killing drug dealers, blowing up drug plants and seizing their financial records. But then the entire unit is needed to take out one plant: Diego Estabon's plant. So, if that package is what you think it is, we're fucked."

"I gotta try to find out what's in that package."

"Felix and the General work for Estabon, and he was Chilly's supplier, right?"

Nick nodded.

"That's something that always has bothered me, Nick, but now it makes sense."

"What's that?"

"Why did Chilly's wife hire us?"

"What do you mean?"

"It's not a hard question. Why did she hire us, a team of paid assassins, for a missing persons case?"

Nick didn't have an answer.

PAYBACK

"I mean, we weren't really private investigators. We didn't advertise, we weren't listed in the phone book, so how did she find us?"

"I never thought about that," Nick said.

"I think that if we could actually find Mrs. Childers, she would tell you that she was recommended by Diego Estabon."

"She does know him, so it's possible," Nick said.

"Who else could it be? They set us up to be killed." Monika paused. "How many people do you think are involved in this?"

"I don't know, Monika. There's no telling how many or how far up the chain of command this goes, but I do know they're still gonna want us dead. That's why I brought you this." Nick handed Monika a wooden box with the initials *M.W.* on it. Monika smiled. The box contained two 9-millimeters. Nick and Jett had given it to her for her last birthday.

"I got them out from your house after you got shot." Nick handed Monika a box of clips. "You should be safe here. Call me if you need me. I promise to answer this time," Nick said and got up.

Chapter Twenty-three

There was no telling what time it was when Shy woke up. At this point, she had no idea what day it was or how long she'd been there. She was being treated well for the most part. *If you can consider being tied to a bed all day treated well.* She considered herself fortunate that she was still alive and hadn't been raped. The only thing she did know was that there was a McDonald's somewhere nearby, or at worst, one of her captors loved it there, because that's all she'd been given to eat.

When it was time for meals, two armed men, both wearing masks and gloves, would come into the room where she was being held. Neither would speak. They would untie her, remove her blindfold and allow her to use the bathroom. While Shy ate, both men would sit in the room with their guns pointed at her. Once she was finished eating, the blindfold was placed over her eyes and they would tie her to the bedpost and leave her alone again.

PAYBACK

Shy slept most of the day, and when she wasn't sleeping, she thought. She tried to think of something constructive, but it wasn't easy to keep a positive mental attitude when she'd been kidnapped and tied to a bed for who knows how many days.

There was one thing that she, no matter how hard she tried, couldn't help thinking about. Who was that woman and why did she want to kill Shy so badly? No matter what she thought about, and Shy had nothing but time to think, she always came back to that one point.

She thought about all the women who might have any reason to want her dead. She had, as a rule, steered clear of women. *They are bad news and bad for business,* Shy remembered her father telling her when she was younger. For that reason, her list of suspects was short. First on her list was Susan, Ricardo's wife. When Shy met Mike, she had been dating Ricardo. But for three years, Ricardo had been living a double life. One night when they were at a club, Ricardo told Shy that he could never see her again because while Shy was in love with him, he had another woman and they were getting married. But then he flipped it on her and told Shy that they could still see each other on the low.

Shy lost her mind. She stood up and pulled out her gun. She was about to kill him, but one of her crew grabbed the gun out of her hand. After that, Shy didn't have any interest in men, preferring instead to concentrate on making money. That was until she met Mike Black.

It didn't take Shy long before she ruled Susan out. She just didn't have it in her.

There was only one person Shy could think of who would have a reason to want her dead. She never actually met her. In fact, she'd only seen her twice, and for the life of her, she couldn't remember her name. Shy remembered the first time she saw her at Impressions on the night that she met Mike. The second time, Shy had just left Mike at Cuisine. She was riding with Jack, one of her old crew, when she saw the woman coming. Shy remembered saying, "Slow down, Jack. I wanna make sure this bitch sees me." They drove past slowly, but the woman wasn't looking. "Honk the horn." When the woman looked at the car, Shy mouthed the words, *He's mine,* then motioned to Jack to drive on.

Shy remembered thinking that it was funny back then. Now, if this was the same woman—*And I'm sure that it is, it couldn't be anybody else*—then it wasn't funny. And if that was the case, then what was whatever her name is doing mixed up with South American drug dealers?

Since the doctor sedated her back on the boat in Miami, she hadn't heard Sal's voice. Was it possible that she was no longer in Miami and that Sal brought her to New York and left her?

New York, Shy thought.

The idea that she might be back home in New York made her smile. Not just because she was in the city, but if she was in the city, Shy knew that sooner or later Mike would find her. It was a very comforting thought.

Just then, Shy heard footsteps coming down the hall and fumbling of keys. She had to laugh at herself, because that sound always made her heart beat faster. She felt like one of Pavlov's dogs, as she knew that sound might mean that she would be allowed to get up and use the bathroom, which, in fact, she had to do soon. Shy listened as the key went into the lock and the door opened.

Once she was untied, Shy got up and stretched. It felt good to get off that bed. Her back was starting to hurt. Shy started to reach for her blindfold.

"Leave that on. We're leaving."

"You're letting me go?" Shy asked.

"Don't ask questions. Just do what you're told and we won't have any problems."

"Can I at least use the bathroom first?"

There was a long pause and then Shy's blindfold was removed. There before her were the same two masked and armed men. "Make it quick."

Once Shy was finished in the bathroom, one of the men told her to put her hands behind her back. Shy complied with their request. After her hands were tied tight and a hood was placed over her head, one of the men said, "Let's go."

They led her out of the room and down four flights of stairs. From the sounds that she heard and the heat, Shy knew she was outside. They walked a little farther then stopped. Shy heard a noise.

I hope that's not what I think it is.

One of the men picked her up and laid her down on something hard. Then she heard the noise that she didn't want to hear: the sound of the trunk slamming. From the time she heard them say that they were leaving, Shy was hoping that it didn't mean she would be riding in the trunk.

Oh well, just one more story to tell the grandchildren. That's when Shy realized that her period was late.

a story by roy glenn

While she was riding in the trunk Shy thought about the men who were holding her captive. She had heard both of them speak. They sounded like they were black, but she couldn't be sure. It made her a little more confident in her earlier assumption that she was no longer in Miami and with the South Americans. But where was she?

When the car stopped and the trunk was opened, one of the men helped Shy out of the trunk and led her into a building. They walked for a while and then stopped. Shy heard an elevator door open. They went up a few floors, and she was led into a room, where she was untied and her hood was removed. Both men backed out of the room and locked the door behind them.

Shy looked around the room she was in. It was definitely a hotel room, but not the best hotel she'd ever been in. In fact, it was probably the worst. The first thing she did was try the door, but it was locked. Next, Shy went to the window to see if she could tell where she was or at least what floor she was on, but the window was bricked shut. She went into the bathroom. "At least it's clean." Shy walked over to the bed, picked up the remote control and turned on the television.

PAYBACK

Chapter Twenty-four

At exactly 5 o'clock, a car pulled into a parking space directly in front of Impressions. The driver, a tall man dressed in jeans and a white T-shirt got out and walked away.

One half-hour later, a woman drove her car into the parking lot and went inside for happy hour. She sat at the bar and ordered a drink.

"Let me have a Hypnotiq, honey." She flirted with the bartender. "You're kinda cute, honey. What's your name." She sat at the bar, drinking and flirting with just about every man who came near her. This went on for the next hour, until a man came in and she invited him to sit down next to her.

The two of them sat at the bar, talking, laughing, dancing and drinking together for hours. At 11:30 the man looked at his watch and whispered, "It's time."

They got up from the bar and walked out of the club arm in arm, still talking and laughing. As they approached the front door, they saw three cops along with the club's security. As they got close enough for everybody to hear, they went into their act.

"You sound like a fuckin' fool," she said as they passed the cops.

"You got that right." The man laughed. "I am a *fuckin'* fool."

At the same time, in the club's office, Tara Wallace, the club's manager, looked at her watch and prepared to make her rounds. She put on her headset and called security. "Greg, meet me in the office. I wanna get my rounds done before the show starts," Tara told him.

"Yeah, P-Harlem is hot. I wanna see him too," Greg said of that evening's entertainment. "I'll be there in a few."

Once Greg arrived, he and Tara went around to all five of the bars in the club and took money from each of the cash registers. A couple of months earlier, Wanda had noticed that profits at the club were down, but the crowds had remained consistent. She brought it up during the monthly meeting with Mike and Bobby. "That means that somebody is stealing," Bobby said.

Wanda handed the income statement to Mike and he looked at the numbers. "Looks more like a whole lotta somebodies stealing, Bob."

"Why don't you have Tara go around during the night with security and count down the registers?" Wanda recommended. "That will at the very least give us better control of the money."

PAYBACK

"If people are gonna steal from you, they'll find a way to do it," Mike said and passed the statement to Bobby. "But I think it's a good idea."

"Glad that's settled," Bobby said and got ready to leave. "I got something that I need to take care of."

"Before you go, Bobby, there's one more thing."

"What's that?" Bobby asked impatiently.

"This funeral home that you said we needed, Mike."

Mike and Bobby looked at one another. "What about it?" Mike asked.

"It's losing money. In fact, it's never made any money. I think that we should cut our losses and sell it," Wanda advised.

"No, Wanda," Mike said. "That funeral home provides a valuable service to the community," he said and followed Bobby out of Wanda's office.

After the registers were counted down, Tara went to the front door and counted that drawer down as well, before returning to the office just before the show started at midnight.

"Good evening, ladies, and welcome to Thursday night live at Impressions. Is everybody havin' a good time?" the MC asked the crowd, but got only a weak response. "I don't believe you heard me. I said is everybody havin' a good time?" This time, the crowd of nearly fifteen hundred people roared. "Is everybody ready for P-Harlem?" The crowd roared again. "That's good, that's good, 'cause we gonna bring him out in just a minute. But before we do that, I wanna remind you all to be sure to tip your bartenders and your waitresses. They are here working hard to take care of you, so you take care of them."

The crowd began to chant, "P, P, P . . ."

a story by roy glenn

"A'ight, a'ight. You've seen him on *106 and Park* and his new single is blowin' up ya radio every day! Impressions very proudly welcomes to the stage, New York's own, P-Harlem!"

The crowd went wild and continued to chant, "P, P, P . . ." as P-Harlem slowly walked across the stage, escorted by two of his dancers, and struck a pose for the crowd. "P, P, P . . ."

"Thank you, Impressions. Thank you," P-Harlem said as he grabbed the mic. "Y'all too good to me."

The chanting continued, "P, P, P . . ."

"Y'all ready to set this bitch on fire?" P-Harlem asked, and the beat began.

Niggaz ain't shit to me.
Truth is, ya crew ain't hot.
Y'all boyz are sloppy, and ya crew don't pop.
We can bang out, let them things out.
My crew don't stop.
How you gangster,
runnin' for safety like Ronnie Lott?

Meanwhile, outside in the parking lot, the argument had begun as planned.

"Who the fuck do you think you talkin' to like that?" the woman yelled. "I'm a muthafuckin' lady, you sorry-ass muthafucka."

"I'm talkin' to you, bitch!" the man yelled back.

"I know you don't think that just because you bought me a few drinks that mean that you gonna get some of this pussy! It takes a whole hell of a lot more than a couple of drinks to get this pussy!" she screamed.

151

PAYBACK

"What do it take then, baby?"

"It takes a lot more than you got," she said and laughed in his face.

"How the fuck you know what I got?"

All I'm tryin' to do is make that cash,
Put it in my stash.
But I see niggaz want me to fail.
I can't do that homie,
Thought I proved that.
New coupe, same color as a taco shell.
Hop out nigga with the stroke,
Bitches ready to fuck.

Outside the club, the argument was beginning to get loud and as expected, one of the officers walked over to see what all the noise was about.

Niggaz looking from the side,
Hatin', approach me on that battle shit.
I was like, what? Go on Fear Factor, *nigga,*
And eat some buffalo nuts,
'Cause this shit's not for you.
See my life; look at the obstacles of Oz.

"Get your muthafuckin' hands off of me!" the woman yelled. As the officer approached, the woman took out her .22-caliber automatic. "I'll kill you!" she screamed and fired two shots at the ground.

Hearing the gunshots, all three officers ran toward the sound, leaving the front door unprotected. The cop, with his gun drawn, yelled, "Drop the gun!" The woman dropped the gun and put her hands up.

a story by roy glenn

"What's goin' on over here?" the cop asked as the other two officers arrived on the scene. They immediately separated the woman from the man.

"Y'all need to lock her up! That bitch is crazy," the man yelled.

"I ain't crazy and I ain't no bitch. This sorry-ass muthafucka was trying to feel on me!"

"So you shot at him?"

"No, I was just trying to scare him with the gun and it went off by accident."

Back inside the club, four armed men in ski masks came though the front door. "Nobody moves and nobody gets hurt." One of the men stayed near the door so he could watch the cops. One of the men moved quickly down the hallway leading to the club. Since the show had everybody's attention, it was easy. One of the robbers put his gun to the security guard's head. "Get down on the floor and don't move or say shit," the gunman instructed.

Youngin' making power moves,
Johnson and Johnson.
You see what that powder do—
Help a nigga stack some Frito Lays.
You need to put ya punks away.
Pitching on the block so long,
I call him Satchel Paige

The fourth man shoved his gun in the face of the woman who was working the register. "Put all the money in the bag and I won't kill you."

The woman quickly complied with the gunman's orders and filled the bag with all the money that was left in the register then handed the bag back to him. With the money in hand, all four bandits backed out the door. Once they were gone, the security guard got up from the ground and called the office on his headset. "Tara, Tara!"

"This is Tara. What's up?"

"We just got robbed."

Chapter Twenty-five

Mike and Bobby made their way though the crowd at Impressions and went upstairs to Bobby's office. The club was still packed. Since the robbery took place during the show, none of the crowd knew about it.

Once they got to the office, Tara explained to them how it went down and how much the bandits came away with. After Tara left the office, they reviewed the front door security tapes. It wasn't too long after that when Nick and Wanda came into the office, together, laughing. It raised an eyebrow, as both Mike and Bobby wondered what they were doing together at this hour of the night.

"What's goin' on?" Nick asked as he and Wanda sat down.

"We got robbed tonight," Bobby answered.

"How much did they get?" Wanda asked.

"Two grand," Bobby told them.

"That's all?" Nick asked.

PAYBACK

"Yeah, we got lucky," Bobby said. "Just before the robbery, Tara took twenty thousand dollars off the front door register."

"Any idea who they were?" Nick asked.

"See for yourself," Bobby said and pointed to the monitor. "There they are."

Nick and Wanda watched the recording of the robbery. Once it was done, Wanda asked, "Where were the police? I don't see the police anywhere."

"They were drawn away from the door by a drunk couple arguing in the parking lot," Bobby told them. "The woman fired a couple of shots and the police came runnin'."

"You think they were in on it?" Nick asked.

"I don't know. The cops told Tara that they just took the gun from her and sent the two of them home."

"You think there's any connection with this robbery and everything else that's goin' on?" Nick asked.

"I don't think so," Bobby said. "What would Curl have to gain by robbing the club?"

"You mean other than money," Nick threw in.

"You're kinda quiet about all this, Mike," Wanda said, noticing that he hadn't said a word since she and Nick came into the office. "What do you think?"

"I don't know what to think about this, Wanda," Mike said and walked over to the bar. "But I will tell you this: the objective wasn't money."

"What makes you say that?" Wanda asked.

"If the objective was money, they woulda waited until the club closed, waited until somebody came out the back door and got all the money from the bars and the door. So, if it is Curl behind this, it would make perfect sense."

a story by roy glenn

"I say again, what makes you says that?" Wanda asked.

"What is Curl trying to do? He is trying to expand his operation. How can he do that? He can only expand by killin' us all and takin' it, or to getting us to sit down with him so we give it to him. At every point, the tactics have been correct, they just weren't executed correctly. Which is why I don't think that it's Curl, or at least it's not him callin' the shots."

"Then who?" Wanda asked as Freeze came through the door.

"Where you been?" Mike asked.

"Yonkers PD."

"Why didn't you call me?" Wanda asked.

"'Cause I wasn't in jail."

"Then what were you doin' there?" Bobby asked.

"Somebody tried to kill me, but they got Pauleen instead. She's dead."

Meanwhile, another meeting was taking place at The Spot between D-Train and the four Impressions bandits. Melinda walked into the office. When she came in, everybody stopped talking and looked at her. She didn't think anything of it. She was used to things like that happening when she entered a room.

"Hi, Dee. How did it go?" she asked.

"Y'all excuse me for a minute," D-Train said to the bandits. They got up slowly and walked out of the office.

Once they were gone, Melinda repeated, "How did it go?"

"Baby, it went just like you said it would," D-Train said as he got up from his desk and put his arms around Melinda. "And this time, everybody did shit according to the plan."

"That's great, baby," Melinda said and kissed him on the cheek. "What about the couple that caused the diversion? Did the cops take them to jail?"

"Nope," he replied and kissed her. "They just took the gun from her and told them both to go home."

"How much did they get?"

"That was the only problem," D-Train said then broke their embrace and started to walk away.

"Oh, Lord, what happened?"

D-Train turned quickly and backhanded Melinda to the floor. "Two fuckin' grand!" he screamed as he stood over her. "My people went through all that shit for two fuckin' grand."

"That's not possible," Melinda said and tried to crawl away from D-Train, but he kept coming.

"Oh, but yes, it is possible, Miss Master Plan."

"I told you that the money wasn't the point. The point was to get them to come to us!" Melinda yelled as she backed herself into a corner.

"Bitch, please. A nigga like Black spend that much on a suit. Them niggas ain't gonna care about losin' two fuckin' grand." D-Train looked at Melinda as tears rolled down her cheeks. "Get up," he said and held out his hand. "Get up. I ain't gonna hit you no more."

"You promise?"

"Yeah, I promise. Besides, I got another problem that I need to deal with." D-Train helped Melinda to her feet and practically dragged her into the stock room. There sat Clark Kent, surrounded by D-Train's crew, gagged, beaten and bloody, tied to a chair.

"What's goin' on here?" Melinda asked.

"This is what happens to a nigga that fucks up."

"What did he do?"

"This dumb bitch decided on his own that he was gonna whack Freeze. But he missed. Killed his woman instead."

"You killed Pauleen?"

"You know her?"

"Of course I know her. We were friends," Melinda said, knowing how fucked up this was. Now there would be no talk. She knew that Freeze would come after them with everything he had. "What are you gonna do with him?"

D-Train took out his gun. "I wanted you to see what happens to niggas that fuck up." D-Train pointed his gun and pumped three shots into Clark Kent's head. "Guess he ain't Superman," D-Train said and his crew laughed. Then he grabbed Melinda by the throat. "You ain't got no more times to fuck up. Understand?"

Melinda said nothing, but understood perfectly. It became very clear to her exactly what she had to do now.

Chapter Twenty-six

Nick arrived at the post office still hadn't heard from Kirk. Since he had been in a hurry to catch Freddie at the post office, Nick allowed Kirk to rush out of his apartment without giving up any information, and now he regretted it. Nick tried to call Kirk again, and again caught Kirk's voicemail. He wanted to call Black and tell him.

Tell him what? That Kirk knew something, but I have no idea what? That I think it has something to do with the DEA? I don't think so. Not after Black just asked me if I was a DEA agent.

Nick needed to run this by somebody and thought that since he wasn't ready to tell Black, Wanda was the next best choice.

The night before, Wanda and Nick talked about his situation for about an hour at her office. After he explained his concerns about what Sally Fitz had told

160

him, Wanda had to agree with him, but she had to ask a question before she said anything else. "Are you DEA, Nick?" Wanda asked with a smile

"No, Wanda, I am not DEA."

"Good for you, Nick. It would break my heart if you were," Wanda said in a somewhat flirtatious way, and then turned serious. "But I agree, you were right to move Monika. How is she doing anyway?"

"She's doin' fine. She just needs to rest. She should be back on her feet in a day or two," Nick told her.

"So, do you think that telling Kirk about Shy was the best idea?"

Nick looked at Wanda.

"I'm just asking because I know that Mike will," Wanda said, but she did question the logic behind it.

Nick smiled. "You mean because he's a cop?"

"Yes, Nick," Wanda said and laughed a little.

"That's exactly why I told him. Look, Kirk hears things we never will. I think he does know something, so I took a chance."

"I hope it pays off, and at worst, doesn't cause us any more problems than it already has. What's bothering me is how Kirk would know or even care about a drug meeting in the Bahamas. Kirk is homicide," Wanda said and looked at the time. "Have you eaten yet?"

"I haven't eaten a thing all day, so I'm starving."

"Well, let's go. I'll buy you dinner," Wanda said and began to gather her things.

"Are you inviting me out on a date?"

"No, Nick, I said that I would buy you dinner. If this was a date, you would be buying me dinner," Wanda said. Nick followed her out of the office.

PAYBACK

After dinner, Nick and Wanda talked over drinks. They talked about business and how she thought Nick could fit in. They were having a good time reminiscing about old times when Wanda noticed that it was getting late. She wanted to see P-Harlem at Impressions. That's when they found out about the robbery and about Pauleen's murder.

Since the bandits only got away with a couple of grand, nobody was overly concerned about the robbery, although the fact that anyone would try it bothered Freeze. He saw it as another challenge to his running of their operation. The real concern was the attempted assassination.

Freeze was sure that D-Train was responsible, and he wanted blood. "I say we go over there now and kill 'em all." But Mike was able to convince him to be sure that D-Train was involved in it before they went to war. So, while Mike and Bobby continued to look for Shy, Freeze went off in search of the owner of a '73 Nova. Nick went to meet Freddie.

When Nick arrived at the post office, Freddie was there waiting for him. He got out and began walking toward him. "How's it goin', Freddie?"

"First of all, let's get one thing straight. You never saw me, so I never talked to you, not today or yesterday. We clear on that?"

"That bad?"

"Are we clear, Nick?"

"I never saw you, Freddie, so we never talked. Now, what you got?"

"Nothing. That's what I got, nothing. All my inquiries were met by a polite brush-off or the word *classified*."

"You have anything for me?"

"Some advice, and this came from Walter."

"How is Walter?"

"Still pissed at you about Beirut. He sends his regards, and said to forget you ever heard any of this."

"Can't do that, Freddie, but thanks anyway for your help. See ya." I started to walk away.

"Back off this one, Nick. It's political."

He stopped in his tracks and walked back to Freddie. "How do you know it's political, Freddie? You know something, Freddie. Give it up."

Freddie stood quietly and looked at Nick. "All right, Nick. Paris did some work for some people we know in Virginia. The word is that it was some white papers that Paris came in contact with, but he was murdered before he got his hands on them."

"Shit, I knew that."

"Sorry you came all this way for nothing," Freddie said, and got back in his car. "Hey, Nick. You ever read a column by Tavia Hawkins?"

"Tavia Hawkins? Who's that?"

"She's a reporter for the *Post*."

"What's she got to do with this?"

"I didn't say she did. Understand? See ya, Nick."

Nick watched Freddie drive away before returning to his car. He drove to the nearest public library and logged on to the Internet. Nick went to the *Post*'s online edition and ran an archive search on Tavia Hawkins. He got ten pages of hits from his search. Nick began reading some of the articles, and it wasn't long before he noticed a pattern. A lot of the articles she'd written lately were about Senator Martin Marshall.

Chapter Twenty-seven

"What you wanna do now?" Bobby asked.

"Let's ride down the Concourse, see what's happening down there," Mike replied. It was getting late in the evening, and Mike and Bobby had been riding all day. They had been to all of the people who usually had information to offer for a price, and still nothing. Nobody knew anything about Shy's kidnapping or knew where they could find Sal Terrico.

Mike had begun to wonder if maybe he'd left the island too soon, or maybe he should have put some pressure on Hector in Miami. No, Shy was in New York somewhere, and he would find her if he had to go house to house to do it. Somebody knew something, saw something. He would just have to find them and make them talk.

They had just come out of a bar when Bobby's cell phone rang and he answered it.

"This is Angelo. Let me talk to Mike."

Bobby told Mike who it was and handed him the phone.

164

"What's up, Angee?"

"Diego called, says he's in town. Says he still wants to meet with you."

"You know what, Angee? This ain't exactly the best time for this shit. I got much more important shit to deal with right now."

"I know this, Mike, but it's a matter of respect, so talk to the guy, get it over with, and get back to what you gotta do," Angelo said.

"That's the thing, Angee. I don't have any fuckin' respect for this guy. I never have. As far as I'm concerned, he's a pussy."

"Look, Mike, so he's not the man his father was in his day."

"Not even fuckin' close, Angee. Gomez was the man. Diego is out of control and fuckin' sloppy, and that makes him dangerous."

"And that's exactly why you need to meet him, hear him out, and if you don't like what he has to say, you can bitch slap his ass again if you wanna."

"What the fuck is he doin' up here, anyway? I know he didn't fly up here just to talk to me about Nick."

"No, he's got business up here. The way I get it, five million dollars worth of legitimate business. Well, kinda legit."

"Yeah, whatever. I still say fuck him."

"Mike! Meet with the fuckin' guy. Get the shit over with before he makes it out to be more than it fuckin' is. Do this for me, okay, Mikey?"

"Okay, as a favor to you. But I don't have time for this. Put him off —"

Bobby interrupted. "Ain't that Manny Valdez over there?" Manny Valdez used to be one of Mike's favorite snitches. Manny would snitch out his mama if there was money in it.

"Yeah, that's him," Mike replied.

"He sees us," Bobby said. "Hey, Manny!"

Manny Valdez looked at Mike and Bobby and took off.

"He's runnin'."

"I'll get back to you, Angee," Mike told him and hung up the phone.

"Why is he runnin'?" Bobby asked.

"I don't know, but let's find out," Mike said and took off running after Manny. Bobby went for his car and drove after them. Mike caught up with him just as Manny made it to his car. Before he could get his key in the ignition, Mike pulled him out of the car.

"Where you goin', Manny?"

"Nowhere, Black," Manny said as Bobby pulled up and got out of the car.

"Why were you runnin' then, Manny?"

"'Cause you said that you would kill me the next time you saw me."

"I did?" Mike questioned. "Why'd I . . . never mind. I'm not goin' to kill you, at least not yet, Manny. I just wanna ask you some questions. Tell me what I wanna know and I won't kill you."

"What do you wanna know? I'll tell you whatever you want. Just don't kill me, Black, please." Manny pleaded for his life.

"You know a guy named Sal Terrico?"

"Yeah, I know Sal. What about him?" Manny asked.

"Where can I find him?" Mike demanded to know.

a story by roy glenn

"What's in it for me?" Manny asked, and with that, Mike punched him in the stomach, knocking the wind out of him. Manny fell to his knees.

While he was still on the ground Mike grabbed him by his collar and slammed Manny's head against the car door. "I already told you what's in it for you, Manny. Tell me what I wanna know and I won't kill you." Mike hit his head against the door again.

"All right, all right, Black. When he's in the city, he likes to get high. Buys his shit from a guy named Red. Runs a shooting gallery out in Queens."

Mike slammed the door against Manny's head again. "I already know that, Manny. Now you tell me where I can find him!"

Bobby leaned over Manny. "Look, Manny, you better tell him something before you end up brain damaged."

"Cityscape!" Manny yelled. "He likes to hang out up there." Manny tried to block the door with his arms, but Mike hit him with the door again and again.

"I know that, Manny. Tell me what I don't know!"

"I know for a fact that he'll be there at two in the morning. He likes to get high with some bitch that dances there. Her name is Jaylyn. She gets off at two. That's all I know, Black, really. Please don't hit me again."

Mike let go of Manny and let his beaten body drop to the ground. "If you see Sal before I do, Manny, I better hear from you," Mike said before walking toward Bobby's car.

After they drove away, Mike turned to Bobby. "We probably just missed him last night."

PAYBACK

"Yeah, but we'll get him tonight. We'll go down there and wait for him. We'll get him tonight, Mike. I promise you that."

"I know, Bobby. I know."

Chapter Twenty-eight

"DEA agent Roman Patterson is murdered in Black's club by associates of Sal Terrico. South American associates. Does any of that relate to those papers? Are those papers about what we did in South America? Then there's Kirk. How does he know what went on in the Bahamas?"

"I don't know, Nick," Wanda said.

"Kirk knows, but all I get from him is voice mail."

"Maybe he'll talk to me. Hold on, Nick." Wanda put him on hold and tried to call Kirk.

When Wanda came back on the line quickly, Nick said, "Voice mail, huh?"

"Yeah."

"What now?"

"I know somebody that we can talk to," Wanda replied. "Meet me at my office in about an hour."

"Why? Who are we going to talk to?"

But Wanda had already hung up.

PAYBACK

Wanda flipped though her Rolodex until she came to the name she was looking for. She dialed the number. "Glynnis Presley, please."

If it involved politics or politicians, Glynnis was the person you wanted to talk to. She was a senator's aide who knew everybody, and more importantly, knew all the inside information about everybody, or at least she could find out. "Everybody talks to somebody that talks to me," Glynnis was famous for saying.

During their long association, Mike Black had been a heavy contributor to a few local political candidates. Any time that he needed to use that type of influence, it was a simple matter to call Glynnis, who called the appropriate congressperson, who made the calls necessary for things to go the way Black wanted them to without any problems.

Before too long she came on the line. "This is Glynnis."

"How you doing, Glynnis? This is Wanda."

"Tired and ready to go home. How about you?"

"I'm fine. I was calling to see if you had any plans for this evening."

"Not a thing. What did you have in mind?"

"Dinner. I got some things that I wanted to run by you."

"Okay, you convinced me."

"Where do you want to meet?" Wanda asked.

"I don't know. What do you have a taste for?"

"I don't know, Italian maybe. Seafood is always good for me," Wanda said. "But let's go someplace that we haven't been before, 'cause you know that I'll go to McCormick and Schmick's and order calamari like I always do. So, what's new and hot?"

"There's a place called Alto on Madison and Fifty-third. They claim that they take Italian food to a new level."

"Have you eaten there?"

"Yes, a couple of weeks ago. It's a nice place, very plush, tall-backed chairs. You'll like it. And the chef comes around and talks with the guests. "

"What about Asian food?"

"I heard of this place called Koi. It's on Fortieth and Sixth Avenue. It's in the Bryant Park Hotel. I hear there's a nice bar there called Cellar Bar."

"Not in the mood for bar hopping, but thanks for the tip." Wanda twirled her pen and thought about it. She always considered every decision carefully. "I think I am feeling Italian."

"Well, how about Bellavitae? It's on Minetta Lane between Sixth Avenue and MacDougal Street. I've never been there, but I hear the food is excellent."

"That's fine. I'll make reservations. Say seven o'clock?"

"Seven is fine with me."

"Oh, and Glynnis, 'there'll be someone joining us for dinner. His name is Nick Simmons. He's an old friend of mine."

"Is he fine as hell and available?"

Knowing what a man-eater Glynnis could be at times, Wanda considered her answer. "Yes, on both counts," she told Glynnis. "But . . . never mind. I'll see you at seven."

As promised, Nick picked up Wanda at her office. She explained that they were going to dinner with Glynnis Presley.

"I take it that this isn't a date either," Nick said.

PAYBACK

"No, this is a business meeting, but are you are more than welcome to pay," Wanda replied.

On the way to the restaurant Wanda explained that Glynnis would be able to fill in some of the holes before they talked to Mike. When they arrived at Bellavitae, Glynnis was already there and had been seated. Wanda introduced Nick to Glynnis and they exchanged pleasantries. Shortly thereafter, the waiter arrived.

"Good evening. My name is Kelly. I'll be your waiter tonight. Our flexible menu allows for light bites or a multi-course feast. I'll give you some time to look over the menu. Can I bring you something from the bar?"

"I'll have a Mojito," Glynnis said.

"Apple martini for me," Wanda said.

"Johnny Walker Black, straight, with a water back," Nick ordered and sent the waiter on his way.

When the waiter returned, he took their orders. Wanda had Fritto Misto.

"That sound good, Wanda. What is it?" Glynnis asked.

"It's calamari with celery, lemon, and caper berries from Salina," the waiter chimed in.

"You always order calamari, Wanda," Glynnis said.

"I love it. What can I say?" Wanda replied and handed the waiter her menu. Glynnis ordered Pollo alla Cacciatora, chicken with black Ligurian olives, while Nick had the grilled pork loin.

During the meal, there was the usual amount of getting-to-know-you small talk between Nick and Glynnis, and plenty of what's-going-on-in-the-city gossip supplied by Glynnis. After dinner, an uncomfortable silence fell over the table.

a story by roy glenn

"So, we've shared a good meal, we've talked a lot of this and that, had some laughs. We've gossiped so much I think we've bored poor Nick to death. And you've plied me with sufficient quantities of alcohol," Glynnis said as she raised her glass. "And I've had such a good time. But you still haven't asked me whatever it is that you invited me here to ask me," she said and signaled for a waiter.

"Maybe we just invited you out to enjoy your company, Glynnis, you know, 'cause we're friends," Wanda said.

"I thought that it was your pretty smile, Glynnis," Nick said and Wanda rolled her eyes.

"You keep talking, honey. I like you," Glynnis flirted. "I imagine that it's you that has the questions."

"What makes you say that?" Nick asked.

"'Cause when Wanda wants to know something, she gets to it over drinks. But you were too polite to even bring it up over dinner."

"All right then, what can you tell me about Martin Marshall?"

"The Justice Department has been investigating Martin Marshall for years."

"For what?" Wanda asked.

"To be honest with you, Wanda, there've been rumors about Marshall and corruption for years. There's even been some talk about him being involved in drug trafficking. Justice even had a bribery case against him three years ago, but the case was dropped."

"What happened?" Nick asked.

"Witness committed suicide."

"How?"

PAYBACK

"Sleeping pills. After that, the evidence that they had disappeared."

"What was the case about?" she asked.

Glynnis paused and thought for a moment. "That case involved drug money."

"How so?" Wanda asked.

"The developer who was *alleged,*" Glynnis was careful to say, "to have offered Marshall the bribe, his partners were drug dealers from Argentina or Brazil or someplace like that."

"Or Peru, maybe?" Nick suggested.

"Could be, but I can't be sure."

"Is there anybody at Justice we can talk to about Marshall?"

"I think I know somebody that could help you," Glynnis said.

"If Justice was investigating him and it involved drugs, then the DEA would have been involved."

"That would only make sense," Glynnis said.

"That would mean that the DEA would have to have at least some knowledge of or be heavy involved in this investigation," Wanda said more to Nick than Glynnis.

"That's a logical conclusion," Glynnis said.

"You have to be pretty powerful to make evidence disappear. Marshall have that kind of power?" Nick asked.

"Marshall has that kind of power. He has a very strong and committed organization. Ruthless, when you get right down to it."

"How does a guy like that continue to get elected?" Wanda asked.

"The thing he's best at is playing the race card— 'The man is hassling me again while I'm out here doing your business, making sure your tax dollars are spent wisely' kinda crap. People buy into it."

"Have you ever heard of a reporter named Tavia Hawkins, Glynnis?"

"Sure I have. She's a reporter for the *Post*. Tavia Hawkins has practically made a career out of writing articles about Marshall."

"So I noticed," Nick said. "I read at least a dozen of them, and there were plenty more. What's up with that? She got it in for this guy?"

"The gossip is that they had an affair. This is years ago. She got serious, wanted him to leave his wife. He dumped her. You know how you men are," Glynnis mused.

"Sounds like she would be a great person to talk to," Nick said.

"If you wanna know about Marshall, she's the one you need to talk to," Glynnis said.

"I wanna go," Wanda said meekly.

PAYBACK

Chapter Twenty-nine

Martin Marshall sat alone at Ben & Jack's Steakhouse on East 44th Street in one of the six private rooms behind etched glass windows off the main dining room. He tapped his fingers on the table and waited impatiently for DeFrancisco to arrive. He hated waiting for him because he was never on time.

There were times when Marshall wished that he'd never gotten involved with DeFrancisco.

If I had to be honest about it, I don't like him.

Aside from always being late, DeFrancisco was arrogant and rude, had the worst table manners of anyone he'd ever known, and to top it off, his breath stank. But he had to admit that despite all of his shortcomings, DeFrancisco had come in very handy over the years.

However, lately DeFrancisco was getting shaky, always worried about things that didn't concern him. He was even reluctant about setting up the sting on Mike Black. He wanted to know why. But who could blame him? Marshall had asked DeFrancisco to commit a considerable amount of DEA resources solely on his assurance that this was important. But Marshall wasn't about to tell him that it was necessary to cover for somebody's fuck-up.

Finally DeFrancisco arrived at the restaurant without any sign of an apology for being late. "Have you ordered yet?" he asked.

"No, I hadn't planned on eating. I asked you here because I needed to talk to you," Marshall replied.

"Well, you don't mind if I do? I haven't had a thing all day and I'm staved." DeFrancisco motioned for the waiter and told him to bring the biggest steak they had, medium well. "And a gin and tonic."

"Anything for you, sir?" the waiter asked Marshall.

"Dewar's on the rocks," Marshall said, knowing that he was going to say what he had to say and be gone before the steak arrived.

Once the waiter was gone, DeFrancisco asked, "So, what do you wanna talk about?"

"I need an update on the Black operation."

"What do you wanna know? The operation is just getting started. The cop, Kirk, reported to them. He seems to be cooperating. By the end of the week, they should be up and running with wiretaps on all of his operations. They're working on picking up cell phone frequencies now, and around-the-clock surveillance on the major players. All that based on the briefing they got from Kirk."

"Make sure they pay close attention to Wanda Moore."

"Who is she?" DeFrancisco asked as the drinks arrived.

"She's their lawyer. Wanda has her hands in everything, both their legal and illegal businesses."

PAYBACK

"All that is fine, Martin, but you still haven't told me what this is all about."

"I've told you all I can tell you, and that is as much for your protection as it is for ours. But I will tell you this: the success of that operation may weigh heavily on your future."

"What's that supposed to mean?" DeFrancisco asked, pressing for information.

"Look, I've told you all I'm going to tell you. You know damn well what I'm saying to you. Both your bank account and your freedom are at stake here. If you can't handle it, I'll get somebody who can."

"Right. You know there ain't nobody gonna do the things I do for you, so let's cut the crap. You need me."

"You're right. We need you to do this and do it right," Marshall said as DeFrancisco's steak arrived. Marshall finished his drink and started to get up.

"There is one more thing I been meaning to tell you," DeFrancisco said as he prepared to dig into his steak.

"What's that?"

"That pain in the ass reporter called me again last week."

"What did she want?"

"Wanted to know if DEA had any knowledge of drug money being involved in the latest investigation against you."

"What did you tell her?"

"Same thing I always tell her. I told her to go fuck herself," DeFrancisco said with his mouth full of steak.

"That's one pain in the ass that neither one of us will have to be bothered with." Marshall stood up, straightened his tie and left the room.

Chapter Thirty

It didn't matter what the captain said. Kirk just couldn't sit on his hands and do nothing. He had to do something, so he decided that the best use of his time was to look into Martin Marshall and his involvement with DeFrancisco.

Kirk had heard that the city's Department of Investigation was looking into a case that involved Marshall, so earlier that day he paid them a visit.

When he arrived at the Department of Investigation, he flashed his badge and was taken to speak with Diane Smith, the head of the department. "DOI is one of the oldest law-enforcement agencies in the country, and an international leader in the effort to combat corruption in public institutions," Diane Smith explained. "It serves the mayor and the people of New York City by acting as an independent and nonpartisan watchdog for New York City government." She was an attractive woman in her early forties, and just a bit of a flirt.

PAYBACK

"What type of cases do you investigate?" Kirk asked.

"DOI's major functions include investigating and referring for prosecution cases of fraud, corruption, and unethical conduct by city employees, contractors and others who receive city money. We also study agency procedures to identify corruption, and recommend improvements in order to reduce the city's vulnerability. We investigate backgrounds of persons selected to work in decision-making or sensitive city jobs, and those who do business with the city, to determine if they are suited to serve the public trust."

"Sounds pretty interesting," Kirk said.

"Oh, please, detective," Diane flirted. "Probably pretty boring compared to the type of cases you get to work on."

"Maybe, but interesting all the same," Kirk flirted back. "All that work must keep you very busy."

"DOI handles at any one time hundreds of complaints," Diane continued. "But in a time of diminishing resources, we continue to find new ways to address the problems challenging the city. But enough about that. Tell me how I can help you, detective."

"I understand that your department is investigating Martin Marshall. Can you tell me anything about that?"

"Our case doesn't involve the senator directly. It's a complaint against a city councilman who is accused of extortion."

"What was the case about?" Kirk asked.

"Allegedly, the councilman and a still unnamed co-conspirator had demanded $1.5 million worth of property and $50,000 cash from a real estate developer who wanted the councilman's vote in favor of a development slated for Brooklyn. We believe that Marshall is his co-conspirator," Diane told him. When Kirk pressed her for more details, she told him that she couldn't give him any more information because the case was still pending. She did, however, refer Kirk to a reporter named Tavia Hawkins, who had written a number of articles on the subject.

Kirk had spent the evening in his new DEA office, reading all of the articles that Tavia Hawkins had written on Marshall. He was on his way home when a call came over the radio about a suicide victim. The woman had taken an overdose of sleeping pills. When he heard that the victim's name was Tavia Hawkins, Kirk just had to drop by and stick his hand in.

When he arrived at her apartment building, most of the other officers and emergency personnel were gone. He was met by one officer, who told Kirk that Tavia Hawkins was reported missing by her editor. It was ruled a suicide when the body was found on the floor in the bedroom, with an empty bottle of sleeping pills by the bed.

"Mind if I have a look around?"

The officer allowed Kirk in the apartment, but stayed with him to make sure no evidence was removed. Kirk searched the apartment, but spent most of his time going through her files and looking at her computer. There was nothing he could find that led him to believe it was anything other than what it appeared to be: the suicidal death of a woman. Tragic, of course, but there was nothing that led Kirk to believe that Tavia Hawkins was murdered.

PAYBACK

Tavia Hawkins was very organized. All of her files, both computer and hard copy, were organized along with her notes, in chronological order according to the story she was working on. She even kept a journal in which she made entries every day. Kirk found volumes of them dating back ten years. What Kirk did find a little strange was that for the last month, there was nothing. No files or notes on what she was working on currently, and the journal was gone. Maybe she ran out of journals, or just stopped making entries. Or maybe she took it to her office. Kirk doubted it, but that in itself was not enough to prove that she was murdered.

Kirk left the apartment and started for his car when he saw Nick and Wanda coming toward him.

"What are you doin' here, Simmons?" Kirk asked.

"I was just about to ask you the same question, Kirk." But Nick knew that if Kirk was here, somebody was dead.

"And in such beautiful company," Kirk added.

"Hello, Kirk." Wanda smiled. She knew Kirk had a thing for her. She had fenced with Kirk many times during his attempts to make a case against Mike Black.

"How are you, Wanda?"

"I'm fine, Kirk, and to answer your question, we're here doing the same thing you are. We came to talk to Tavia Hawkins," Wanda said and Nick gave her a look.

"That's not gonna happen."

"Why not?" Wanda asked.

"'Cause she's dead."

"Murdered?" Wanda asked.

"Suicide."

Nick and Wanda looked at one another. Wanda started to say something, but Nick cut her off. "That's too bad, Kirk," he said and grabbed Wanda by the hand. "Good night, Kirk." Nick and Wanda started walking back to his car, with Kirk following behind them.

"What did you want to ask her about?"

"Doesn't matter now, does it, Kirk?" Nick said.

"No, it doesn't, but I'm just curious."

When they got to his car, Nick got in quickly while Wanda played off Kirk. "Have you any reason to detain us, detective?"

"No, just curious."

Wanda smiled. "Then I'll say good night."

Kirk opened her car door and Wanda got in. "Good night, Wanda," he said and closed her door.

Chapter Thirty-one

"What the fuck are you talkin' about?"

"You know what I'm talkin' about, Bobby. I'm tired of that bitch callin' my house talkin' stupid. Make the bitch stop, Bobby, or I'll stop her," Pam said and hung up the phone.

Bobby looked at Mike. "I don't have time to talk about this now. I'll call you later," he said to nobody as he parked in front of Cuisine.

"Pam sounds mad," Mike said as he got out of the car and headed inside the club.

Bobby followed behind him. "Yeah."

"Handle your business."

When Mike and Bobby got to the office, Wanda and Nick were already there. "I think we need to talk," Wanda said.

"What about?" Mike asked.

"I've been trying to get more information about those papers and what's in them," Nick said.

"And?" Mike asked.

"I'm starting to think I was right. Those papers are about what went on in South America. I checked with

184

an old source of mine and he put me on to a reporter who writes a lot of articles about Senator Martin Marshall."

"What does Marshall have to do with any of this?" Mike asked.

"My source tells me that Marshall is rumored to be connected to a South American drug dealer," Wanda said, excited to finally be a part of something while it was going on and not just having to clean up the mess afterwards.

Mike smiled at her. "Who told you that, Glynnis?"

"Yes," Wanda said and smiled back.

"She's right. Marshall's been mixed up with Diego for years." Mike looked at Nick then he looked at Wanda sitting next to him. "I'm thinking that Diego might have his hands in a lot of shit."

"It was Diego's operation we were movin' on when the rest of my unit was killed," Nick said. "Those papers surfacing, their connection to Diego, may be his connection to Marshall."

"You think it's Diego that's backin' D-Train in this move he's making against us?" Bobby asked.

"Don't it all make perfect sense to you? Don't you see how all the pieces are falling into place?" Mike said to a group of puzzled faces. "Let me break it down for you."

"This oughta be good," Bobby said and sat next to Mike.

"You see, Nick, it all begins with you. You were down there eliminating all of Diego's competition."

"But when it came time to take out Diego's operation, the whole unit is killed," Nick said.

"Eliminate the eliminators," Wanda said.

PAYBACK

"You and your team survived, but Diego still needs you dead. So, along comes Chilly's wife, and she distracts you with her legs and that business of hers. One of two things were bound to happen. One, Chilly kills you for involving yourself in his business."

"Which he tried," Nick said.

"Or you team is so distracted with Chilly that they don't see the hit coming."

"Which they did," Wanda threw in.

"Only Monika survives," Nick said. "And Freeze kills Felix and the General."

"But Diego's objective hasn't changed," Mike said quickly. "He still needs to kill you and Monika."

"Only now he has a greater sense of urgency because he hasn't gotten his hands on those papers."

Mike looked at Bobby, who had been unusually quiet. "You know what, Mike?"

"What's that Bobby?"

"That's sounds all good, and the shit makes perfect sense and all fits together so nice and neat and all that shit, but would you like to know what I think is goin' on?"

"What do you think is goin' on, Bobby?" Mike asked.

"This oughta be good," Wanda whispered to Nick.

"I heard that, Wanda," Bobby said without looking her way. "I think Diego is still mad 'cause you bitch slapped him and he ended up going to jail behind it."

Mike laughed and Nick and Wanda looked confused. "I never heard this story," Wanda said. "But there's nothing new about that."

"Neither have I," Nick said.

186

"'Cause there's nothing to tell," Mike said, but he was still laughing a little. He turned to Bobby. "You think that's what this is all about?"

"Yes," Bobby said definitely. "I do." But then he started laughing too.

"Well, are you gonna tell us what happened or do we have to guess?" Wanda asked, but by this time, she was laughing too.

"This was a long time ago, back when me and Mike were still collecting for André and Hector used to buy from him. Hector was a little slow payin', which wasn't any big deal. Hector was a stand-up guy. When he had the money, he always paid. But André didn't like Hector, and wanted me and Mike to lean on him. So, we go around to this bar Hector hung out in and have our usual you're-late conversation with Hector, and Diego's there."

"You gotta remember, back then, Diego was just Gomez's punk, fresh off the boat from Peru, tryin' to make a rep," Mike said as Freeze came into the office.

"Don't try to clean that shit up now, nigga. I'm tellin' this story," Bobby said.

"What y'all talkin' about?"

"Don't interrupt me when I'm talkin'. That shit is just plain fuckin' rude," Bobby said to Freeze, who put up his hands in surrender. "So, Mike is talkin' shit to Hector like he always does, but Diego hears him and rolls up behind Mike, and say some shit like, 'Why you comin' up in here, talkin' shit like you all bad and shit?' or some shit like that. Mike doesn't even look back. He just wheels and backhands Diego to the ground. Then Mike stands over him and says, 'I wasn't talkin' to you,' and goes back to talkin' to Hector like it wasn't shit.

"So, Diego gets up from the floor and leaves the bar, but by now, everybody in the place is laughing at him. Now, I guess he went and got a gun, and the cops see him with it. I don't know. But anyway, they stop him, and when they search the car, Diego's carryin'. I forget how much, but it was enough to get him ten years. He did two and went back to Peru when he got out."

"That may be part of it, Bobby, but there's got to be more to it than that," Mike said.

"So, what you wanna do now, Black?" Freeze asked.

"Let's go get Sal Terrico."

Chapter Thirty-two

Mike had gotten in the car with Bobby when he noticed that Wanda was getting in the back seat of the truck with Nick and Freeze. "I'll be right back."

Mike walked over to the truck and Freeze rolled down the window. Mike knocked on Wanda's window. She cursed and rolled down her window to see what he wanted, but she already knew. "Where do you think you're goin', counselor?"

"With y'all," Wanda said quietly, while Freeze dropped his head and Nick looked out the window.

Mike paused for a moment and then he smiled. "She's your responsibility, Nick," he said and walked back to the car.

When they arrived at Cityscape, it was almost 1:30 in the morning. They made their way up the steps and into the strip club.

Once they had looked around and were sure that Sal wasn't there, they took up positions around the club. Since neither Bobby nor Freeze had ever seen Sal Terrico, they covered the exits to make sure that he couldn't get away once he was in there. Nick and Wanda took a seat near the stage, where Nick could see the door. Mike sat at a table in the back so he could see the whole club.

Mike signaled for a waitress, but a dancer responded to his motion. "How you doin tonight? You want a table dance?"

"I was tryin' to get a drink," Mike said.

"I'll send a waitress over," the dancer said and started to walk away.

"Hey!" Mike shouted. "Is there a dancer here called Jaylyn?"

"Yeah," the dancer said and looked around. "There she go, right there. You want me to send her over?" She pointed to a dancer dressed in just enough black leather to cover the more sensitive areas. Jaylyn was a pretty woman, about five feet eight inches tall, with a small waistline, deep brown skin, dark brown bedroom eyes and shoulder-length black hair, just like Shy.

"No." Mike reached in his pocket and peeled off a twenty. "Just send the waitress."

"My name is Diamond Princess," the dancer said, looking at Mike and the wad of money. "You let me know if you need anything."

On the other side of the club, Nick was looking at Wanda, who was looking at him. "What?" Wanda asked over the music.

Nick leaned closer. "Just wondering if you're having a good time."

"Yes. I'm just glad to be here," Wanda said, nodding her head to the music. "Not that watching these women parade around naked is any big deal. I can see this at any one of the houses. I'm just glad to be hangin' out with you guys, you know, like we used to. I miss that. Do you know how it feels to find out everything the day after or maybe years after? Mike is so overprotective of me." Wanda took a sip of her drink. "But I guess it's for the best."

"So, I guess we can't call this a date either," Nick said in Wanda's ear. It had become sort of a running joke between them, but after spending the last two nights with Wanda, he was beginning to think that maybe it wasn't such a bad idea.

Wanda smiled and took another sip before answering. "No, Nick, this is definitely not my idea of a date."

"It's not? Well then, tell me what is your idea of a date, Wanda?" Since the time he was working for Chilly's wife, when Wanda bailed him out of jail and he spent the night telling her his story, Nick had been watching her. Wanda was tall and slender, but thick with it in all the important areas.

"Let's see, my idea of a date," Wanda began.

"Hold up," Nick said and stood up. "That's him. Wait here."

Nick moved toward Sal Terrico, who was pushing his way through the crowd toward Jaylyn. He pointed Sal out to Mike, and he signaled Bobby and Freeze.

Sal stopped dead in his tracks. Even though Mike and Bobby didn't remember him, Sal recognized Bobby and knew that Mike Black couldn't be far away.

Sal looked around quickly for a way out. That's when he felt the gun in his back.

"Hello, Sal," Mike said and patted Sal down. "I've been waiting for you," he said and took Sal's gun. "Come on, Sal. Let's talk outside." Mike told Freeze to put Wanda in a cab.

PAYBACK

As soon as they got down the steps and outside the club, Sal started talking. "Listen, Black, I never wanted to take her. We just needed her to get outta there. I swear to God, Black, I didn't know that she was your wife or that it was your spot," Sal told him quickly as they walked him around the corner. Bobby and Freeze pulled out their guns and pointed them at Sal. Mike grabbed him by the throat. "When she told me who she was, I wanted to let her go, but Papi said to take her to Miami."

"Papi? Who the fuck is Papi?"

"Diego, Diego Estabon." Mike let Sal go. "When we got to Miami, he said to bring her here. I dropped her where he told me."

"Where was that?" Mike asked.

"I dropped her at an apartment on a Hundred and Fifty-first Street. They took her from there."

Freeze punched Sal in the face. Bobby grabbed him before he fell. "They? Who the fuck is they?" Freeze yelled.

"I don't know who the guys were. I just dropped her and got away from there."

Freeze hit Sal again while Bobby held him. "Take us there," Mike demanded.

On the way to Harlem, Bobby drove, Nick sat in the front seat with his gun pointed at Sal. Mike and Freeze were in the back seat on either side of Sal.

"You don't have to worry, Sal. I'm not gonna kill you, at least not yet," Mike said calmly. "I just need you to clear some things up for me."

"Sure, Black, whatever you need."

"Who set the meeting in my club?"

"Pat, Pat Matthews."

"Who is that? The one Julio shot?"

192

"Yeah," Sal answered nervously.

"Why'd Julio kill him?"

"Julio said he was DEA."

"Is that why Julio shot at him, 'cause he was DEA too?" Mike asked, pointing in Nick's direction.

Sal glanced at Nick then turned back to Mike. "He's not the one Julio was shooting at, but yeah, he was with them. I mean, it was just him and your wife shooting at us."

"So, Julio recognized another agent and that's who he shot at?" Mike asked.

"Yeah. After they started shooting at us, we grabbed her to get outta there. I swear to God, Black, that's what happened."

When they arrived at 151st Street, Sal told them that he took Shy to an apartment on the fourth floor. Bobby parked the car down the block from the building, while Freeze and Nick went to check things out. They went inside and took the back staircase to the fourth floor. Once Nick confirmed that there was nobody in the hallway, he called Mike.

Mike and Bobby led Sal into the building at gunpoint. They took the elevator up to the fourth floor where Nick and Freeze were waiting. Mike told Nick to watch Sal as he and Bobby approached the door. Mike kicked in the door and Bobby and Freeze rushed inside the apartment, but it was empty. While Bobby and Freeze searched the apartment, Mike put a silencer on his gun.

"Black, take a look at this," Freeze said and led Mike into one of the rooms. There was a bed in the room with ropes tied to the four posts.

PAYBACK

"She was here," Mike said. "Bring him in here, Nick."

Nick pushed Sal in the room. "This is where I brought her, Black. I swear."

"Where did they take her?" Mike yelled and pointed his gun at Sal.

"I don't know!"

Mike lowered his weapon. "As soon as she told you she was my wife, you should have let her out the car and apologized for taking her," Mike said and raised the gun again. He shot Sal twice in the head.

Chapter Thirty-three

The next afternoon, Mike asked everybody to meet him at Cuisine. Freeze arrived first. "What's up, Black?" he asked and sat down at the table with Mike.

"What's up?"

"Chillin'," Freeze said.

"What about that thing for Pauleen? What's up with that?"

"I got that. I am gonna take care of it today," Freeze said.

"I don't want you goin' alone, so wait for me or take Bobby with you."

"If I can find him," Freeze commented.

"What's up with him and this chick anyway?"

"Black, the shit is out of control. I know I should have told you about it sooner, but I gave Bobby my word. But that bitch is crazy. I'm sorry I introduced him to her. She's a bad bitch, but I didn't think Bobby was gonna lose his fuckin' mind over her. It's gotten to the point that Pam knows about it."

"How you know that?"

195

PAYBACK

"'Cause Pam be callin' me lookin' for that nigga," Freeze said excitedly. "Pam be callin' me talkin' 'bout, 'Where's Bobby? Is Bobby with you at the club? He said he was at Cynt's, but I just talked to Cynt and she ain't seen him.' I'm gettin' fuckin' tired of that shit. You need to talk to him, but I don't know if that shit will do any good, as far gone as that nigga is, Black."

"I'll talk to him," Mike said as Bobby walked in. "You handle what you gotta handle, but watch your back. You know what I'm sayin'?"

"You know what a careful guy I am," Freeze said and thought about Pauleen. If he had been more careful that day, maybe . . .

"How's Nick's partner? What's her name again?"

"Monika. She's doin' a'ight for somebody who took five shots. She coulda walked out of the hospital, but they made her use the wheelchair."

"She with our friend in Mount Vernon?" That was Mike's way of asking if Monika was with Perry. He was a part of the crew until Bobby paid for him to go to medical school. Now he ran a small practice in Mount Vernon with his wife.

"He'll take good care of her."

"You talk to her?"

"A little," Freeze said.

"What you think of her?"

"She's Wanda with guns."

"Who y'all talkin' about?" Bobby asked.

"Nick's partner, Monika," Freeze told him.

At that moment, Wanda and Nick arrived and sat down.

"The big question is why is the DEA settin' up meetings in my club?"

"I'll tell you what I think," Wanda said. "I think it was to make it look like you—and more importantly, Shy, a known drug dealer with a warrant for conspiracy to distribute—were involved in the meeting."

"Exactly," Mike said. "Julio was shooting at another DEA agent. They had an operation up and running."

"That's why the DEA never sent an investigator to the club," Wanda said.

"Because they were there. That agent wouldn't be in there without backup," Mike said.

"But if that's true, Mike, and there were other agents there, when the shooting started, why wouldn't they get involved?" Wanda asked. "Especially after their agent was killed."

"Because Sal Terrico and his friends weren't the objective. If Black was the objective, an undercover operative gettin' killed wasn't a reason to blow the operation," Nick said. "If Black were there, maybe then they would have waited until the shooting stopped and arrested him."

"See, I knew you were smart enough to follow me," Mike said. "Wanda, I need to know for sure if the DEA is on us. And find out exactly why they're on us."

"I'll make some calls first thing in the morning."

"Nick, you stay on this thing with Marshall. See if you can find out the real deal with those damn papers. And if he is responsible for that reporter's death, I wanna know about it."

"What about Kirk?" Nick asked.

"Stay away from Kirk, but I think Kirk is working the same thing from a different angle."

PAYBACK

Bobby turned to Mike. "We need to think about where we wanna go from here. They're coming at us from all sides now. D-Train tryin' to take us one way, DEA might be at us and who knows what Diego's sneaky ass is up to. Maybe it's time for us to get out."

Mike looked at Bobby. He was thinking the same thing. "Maybe it is," Mike said quietly.

"And if that's what's gotta happen, then that's what's gonna happen," Bobby said.

"Or we could kill them all," Mike said, "and then get out. But somehow, Bobby, I don't think just killin' Diego is gonna satisfy me."

Wanda rolled her eyes. "I'm just gonna throw this out there. I know we need to find Shy, but after that, we don't need to do this. We're making almost as much money in our legitimate businesses as we do with everything else that we have going on." Wanda looked around the table. "Everyone at this table is a millionaire. I think Bobby is right. It's time for us to get out."

"I just don't like the idea of gettin' pushed out like this," Bobby said.

"I'm not sayin' that either of you are wrong. In fact, I agree with you. We don't need to live like this, but we can't just walk away. Not from this. Sure, we can let D-Train have the houses, and we can put a stop to whatever Diego is up to, but we can't just walk away from the DEA. If we do nothing, they'll still come."

"But if we're not involved in anything what will they have?" Wanda asked.

"We're not *involved* in anything now, and here they are. No, Wanda, we got to get the DEA off us."

Chapter Thirty-four

Nick banged on the door for a good while before Freeze opened the door.

"Knew it was you, Nick," Freeze said.

"I thought you were 'sleep," Nick said and walked in the apartment.

"Nope, but I'm glad you're here. Now you can ride with me."

"Where we goin'?"

"We gonna knock on a few doors, ask a few questions, maybe kill a muthafucka or two."

"What's up?"

"Black wanted me to wait for him or Bobby before I go ride on the muthafucka that killed Pauleen, but Black's still looking for Shy, and Bobby's ass is nowhere to be found."

"Fuck that," Nick said. "This is the way it should be. Me and you, like old times. Ride or die, right," Nick said and held out his hand.

PAYBACK

Freeze grabbed his hand hard and shook it. "Glad to have you back, Nick," he said as the two walked out to the car.

Once they were on their way, Nick's cell phone rang. "Hello," he answered.

"Hello, Nick, this is Wanda. How are you?"

"I'm fine, Wanda. What about you? Are you havin' a good day?" Nick asked.

"So far so good. What are you doing?"

Nick glanced over at Freeze as he drove, nodding his head to the beat. "I'm ridin' with Freeze."

"Oh," Wanda said. "Well, I'm not going to keep you. I have two things to tell you."

"What's that?"

"I was able to confirm that there is an ongoing operation, but I wasn't able to get a feel for the scope of it."

"Did you tell Black?"

"Yes."

"What did he say?"

"He said, 'That's nice. I'll talk to you later.' "

Nick laughed a little. "Okay, what's the second?"

"Our friend Martin Marshall is having a black tie affair at his house tomorrow night. Glynnis says she can get us invitations. You interested?"

"Of course," Nick said and then he thought about it. He started to ask if this was a date, but he looked at Freeze and decided against it. "See if you can get another invite."

"Who are you talking about bringing? Not Freeze, I hope."

"No. if she's up to it, I'd like Monika to come with us," Nick said. He thought he heard Wanda sucking her teeth, but chose not to mention it.

"I'll see what I can do," Wanda said, ready to hang up the phone.

"Make that happen, Wanda. Her being there is important to what I need to do."

"I'll get it done, Nick. No problem."

Nick hung up the phone.

Freeze looked at Nick. "I don't mean to get in your business, Nick, but what's up with you and Wanda?"

"What do you mean?"

Freeze laughed. "Okay, that how you wanna carry me after all that ride or die shit."

"I don't know what you're talkin' about. There's nothin' goin' on between me and Wanda."

"You forget who you was talkin' to, nigga? You may be able to run some of that weak shit past Bobby or whatever, but I know better. I know you."

"You know better, huh?"

"Yeah, I know. So you can tell Black and them whatever you want to, but you and I know what's goin' on," Freeze said, smiling as he drove.

"Why don't you tell me what's goin' on with me and Wanda?"

"You fuckin' her. And if you ain't, you gonna."

"How you know all this?"

"I was watchin' the two of you last night."

"What were we doin'?"

"Nick, where were we last night?"

"Cityscape."

"And what is Cityscape?"

"It's a tittie bar."

"Exactly. You sittin' in a room full of naked woman, I mean titties everywhere, and what you doin', huh?"

"What was I doin'?"

PAYBACK

"You were all up in Wanda's face, and she's all up in yours. Gigglin'. Fuckin' Wanda was all up in your grill, gigglin' her ass off. I ain't never seen Wanda all bouncy and gigglin' the whole time I known her."

"That don't mean nothing. I was watchin' the dancers too," Nick offered meekly.

"Yeah, whatever, kid. Sure you were. But I ain't mad at you at all. Wanda's a fine muthafucka. Somebody need to bust that body. It might even chill her ass out if she start gettin' some dick on the regular."

"You think so?"

"Yeah, so I ain't mad at you at all, Nick."

"Then why you fuckin' with me?" Nick asked and looked out the window. If he wanted to be honest with himself, he was really starting to feel Wanda. And for maybe the first time in his life, he was intimidated by a woman. Wanda was strong-willed and powerful. That's what turned him on. He'd been tempted to ask her out and probably would have at Cityscape, but Sal Terrico came into the club.

Nick's plan for the day was to drop by and invite Wanda to join him at this little Mediterranean joint he'd been eyeing. He'd been looking forward to it all day, but for some reason, he decided to check on Freeze first.

You know, be there for a brother who just lost his woman. But when you really sit and think about it, that's exactly what I'm doin'. Freeze ain't the type of guy that was gonna be sittin' around depressed and feelin' sorry for himself. Pauleen's funeral will be in a day or two, and her killer has to be dead before she can rest in peace.

a story by roy glenn

Freeze had just turned down Willett Avenue when he saw it. "There it is, Nick. Beat to shit '73 Chevy Nova." Freeze got out of his truck and put his hand on the hood of the car. "It's still warm." One of his snitches told Freeze that the name of the man that killed Pauleen was Paul Clay, and he told Freeze where he lived

While Nick approached the house cautiously, Freeze walked boldly to the front door and beat on it like he was the police.

The door swung open. "What is it now?" the man said angrily. "Who the fuck are you?" he asked when he realized that it wasn't the police.

"You Paul Clay?"

"Who the fuck are you?"

Freeze looked at Nick and shoved the man inside the house. He fell to the floor. Both Freeze and Nick had their guns drawn and pointed at the man. "You Paul Clay?" Freeze asked again.

"No. I'm his brother," he said, trying to inch away from Freeze and Nick.

"Where is he?"

"He's dead."

"Who killed him?" Freeze demanded to know.

"I don't know. The last time I saw him, he told me some shit about how he may die for love. Next day, he was dead."

Freeze dropped his head and turned away.

"What did he mean by that?" Nick asked.

"He was fuckin' around with somebody woman. I guess the guy got Paul first."

PAYBACK

Nick watched Freeze walk out of the house. "Sorry to bother you," he said and followed Freeze to his truck.

Once they were in the truck and had driven away, Nick turned to Freeze. "You already knew about Pauleen, didn't you?"

Freeze nodded.

"It wasn't the first time either, was it?"

Freeze shook his head.

"So, if you didn't kill him, who did?"

"I don't know, Nick," Freeze said quietly.

"What were you expecting to find here?"

"What you mean?"

"I mean, we know that the guy was tryin' to shoot you and shot Pauleen. Do you think this guy was tryin' to kill you over her, or was he a soldier for your boy Curl?"

Freeze banged the steering wheel. "I don't know, Nick. Just shut the fuck up and let me think for a minute, okay?"

"Lighten up, man. This is between me and you, and that's where this stays, me and you. Nobody has to know."

For the next few blocks, they drove in silence. "You ever know something, but it's still hard to hear?"

"Yeah," was all Nick could say. "Yeah, I know what you mean."

"But you know what, Nick? I ain't got time for that shit now. We got work to do."

"That's what I'm sayin'. So, you think this nigga was one of your boy's soldiers?"

"Not that it matters, 'cause I was fuckin' everybody too, but she was fuckin' everybody. I really needed to be done with her ass a long time ago."

"Why didn't you?"

"I ain't even gonna front. Pussy was all that, Nick. She just liked to fuck all the damn time. Her ass get mad, damn near ignorant when she don't get no dick."

"I know what that's like," Nick said and thought about Camille.

Freeze started to laugh as he thought about Camille too. "Yeah, I guess you do."

Nick laughed.

"But you see, Nick, that's how things turn around. Now it's Bobby that's losin' his mind over some little trick."

"Yeah, what's up with that?"

"Bobby ran up on a little dancer got him pussy whipped, that's all. Why? You wanna meet her?"

"Oh, hell no. I don't need to get nowhere near anybody Bobby fuckin' with no more in life."

"I'm just fuckin' wit' you, Nick. That bitch crazy anyway. I hate I introduced him to her."

"Anyway," Nick said, trying to end the discussion. "What you gonna do now?"

"I know you got a date with Wanda and shit."

"It's not a date," Nick interrupted quickly.

"Whatever, Nick. So, I'm gonna roll you back to your car."

"What you gonna do?"

"I'm gonna find out if that nigga worked for Curl."

"And if he did?"

"I'm gonna wait for you or Black or Bobby before I go kill him."

Chapter Thirty-five

Bobby parked his car across the street from Angelo's, and he and Mike went inside. Diego finally called and was ready to meet. As always, they were met by Jimmy, who escorted them to a private room just off the bar area. Inside the room was a table and five chairs.

Once they made themselves comfortable, Angelo came into the room with a bottle and three glasses. "Mike, Bobby, how's everybody doin'?" He took a seat at the head of the table. "As you can see, Diego is even later than you are."

"Diego had Shy all along. That shit with Nick was just a cover," Mike told Angelo.

"You're fuckin' kiddin' me," Angelo said and poured himself a drink.

"We caught up with Sal Terrico last night. Diego told him to bring her here."

Bobby took the bottle from Angelo. He poured himself a drink and one for Mike. "How you wanna play this, Mike?" he asked.

"I'm not gonna let on that I know he has her. Let him lay it out any way he wants—"

Mike was interrupted by a knock at the door.

"Come on," Angelo yelled.

Jimmy opened the door and showed Diego Estabon into the room. "Get two more glasses, Jimmy," he said as Diego walked toward him, followed by another man. "Diego, how are you?" Angelo said as the two men embraced.

"Very well, thank you, Angelo." Diego turned to Mike. "Mike Black, my old friend, it has been too long. You must come to Lima some day soon and let me show you how we live."

Mike stood up and embraced Diego. "Like the king that you are Diego, my friend."

Bobby shook his head in disgust but offered a hand. "How you doin', Diego?"

"Like Mike said; like a king, Bobby," Diego said and tightened his grip. "Like a king."

Once everyone had taken a seat, Angelo asked, "So tell me, Diego, what can I do for you today?"

Diego paused and looked at Angelo. "For me, nothing." Diego turned to Mike. "Today there is something that I can do for you, Black."

"You have my undivided attention," Mike said, trying to sound as gracious as he could.

"I heard about that unfortunate business that went on in your club."

"Bad news travels fast," Mike said and leaned forward.

"A man in my position, I hear things, things that only men like us are in a position to do something about. This is what I have done for you, my friend.

PAYBACK

When it came to my attention that your wife was taken, I took steps to intervene on your behalf."

"So, what are you sayin', Diego?" Angelo asked. "Are you sayin' that you got Shy?"

"I was able to use my influence to assure her abductor that our business is not your business, and that appearances to the contrary, they have nothing to fear from you. They have assured me that your wife has not been harmed, and she will be released."

"When?" was Mike's single word question.

"Tonight at Penn Station." Diego looked at his watch. "At ten o'clock, which is in thirty minutes."

"Bobby."

Bobby took out his cell phone and called Freeze to have somebody get down to Penn station as soon as possible. Mike's eyes narrowed as he continued to stare at Diego.

"I am sorry about the short notice, my friend," Diego said.

"Yeah, I was just about to mention that," Angelo interjected. "You coulda told me and he coulda had somebody there to meet her."

"This is true. Somebody could have met the woman and perhaps killed them in retaliation. I'm sure her abductor considered that possibility very carefully when he negotiated that point." Diego turned to Mike. "What can be done to make this right?"

"What about her abductor?" Mike asked, knowing that he'd already killed Sal and Julio.

"You have my word that they will be dealt with once her safe return has been established."

"Turn them over to me," Mike demanded.

"If I were to do that, would you kill them?"

"Yes, Diego, I will kill him, and anyone I find who was involved in it."

"Why, when your wife is unharmed and to my knowledge has been well treated?" Diego asked.

"He's got a point, Mike," Angelo had to agree.

"Okay, Angelo," Mike said. "I'm a reasonable man, and I want to take care of this in a reasonable manner. I'm sure that you understand my anger and my desire for revenge, but out of respect for you, Angelo," Mike paused long enough to make his point. "I will not seek retribution in this matter of disrespect."

"I am very glad to hear that," Diego said and got to his feet quickly. "Now that the matter is dispensed with, I have some business that I must attend to. Please let me know if things do not happen in the manner that we have discussed," he said as he walked to the door. Then he stopped. "And please let me know if there is ever anything that I can do for you." And with that, Diego Estabon closed the door and was gone.

"Can you get somebody to follow him, Angee?"

"I'm on it," Angelo said and left the room.

"What you gonna do now?" Bobby asked as he and Mike got up from the table.

"I'm going to make sure that Cassandra is safe, then I'm gonna kill him and anyone I find who was involved in it."

"You just told Diego that you wouldn't do that," Bobby said and laughed.

"Fuck Diego."

Chapter Thirty-six

Shy lay across her bed and watched *Law and Order* on television. She'd never seen it before and was actually pretty surprised at how much she was enjoying it.

She heard keys in the lock and got off the bed. The door opened and as usual, the same two men walked in. One threw Shy a hood. "Put that on and then hold your hands out in front of you. We're goin'."

Shy quietly complied with their orders and her hands were quickly tied in front of her. They led her out of the room and down the stairs. On the way down, Shy prepared herself for another ride in the trunk.

It wasn't all that bad once you get past the idea of it, Shy thought.

So, she was pleasantly surprised when she heard the words, "You're gettin' in the car, so watch your head." One of the men gently pushed Shy's head down.

a story by roy glenn

As the car moved, Shy gave some thought to where she was going and what she could expect when she got there. Suddenly, the car stopped.

"Hold out your hands."

Shy did as she was told then felt him tugging on the rope. Next Shy felt the man reach across her and she heard the door open. "Get out," he said and gave Shy a push. She stumbled out of the car and quickly pulled off her hood in time to see a taxi speed away and get lost in a sea of cabs. It didn't matter; she was free.

Shy looked around to see where she was, and a smile came across her face when she realized that she was standing outside Penn Station. She was home. Shy very happily began to walk down 34th Street toward Seventh Avenue, but stopped in her tracks when she saw two cops standing on the corner. At that moment, she got very paranoid when she thought about the fact that she had an outstanding warrant.

Slowly, she came to the conclusion that she wasn't on *America's Most Wanted* and every cop in New York wasn't out looking for her, so she calmed down a little. Her next thought was about what she should do. There was no way for her to know if anybody knew that she was free, much less if anyone was coming to pick her up.

Okay, you wanted to be back in New York, big girl, so what now?

Shy knew that the first thing she needed to do was to call somebody and let them know that she was all right, but she had no money.

Shy walked down the street looking at the people as they passed, until she saw a sympathetic-looking

211

woman sitting on some steps outside Penn Station. She was talking on her cell phone. Shy walked over and stood near the woman, waiting patiently for her to finish her call.

"Excuse me," Shy said, and the woman turned to her. "I don't mean to bother you, but can I use your cell phone, please? I'm stranded, and I need to call somebody to come and get me. I promise I won't take long."

The woman passed Shy the phone. "Take your time, honey."

Shy thanked the woman and dialed a number.

"Cuisine, how may I direct your call?" the receptionist asked.

"May I speak to Mike Black, please?"

"Mr. Black is not in. Can somebody else help you?"

"What about Bobby Ray?"

"Mr. Ray is not in either."

"This is Cassandra Black. Is Freeze or Wanda there?"

"Mrs. Black, are you all right?" the receptionist asked.

"I'm fine."

"Where are you?"

"I'm on Thirty-fourth Street outside the Garden."

"That's good. Stay right where you are. Freeze is on his way to get you. Hold on, and I'll find out how long he'll be."

"Thank you, but please hurry. I'm on somebody's cell phone."

"I won't be long, I promise," the receptionist said and put Shy on hold.

"No need to rush. Take your time, honey. I know how niggas get when you don't give them what they want. I saw them push you out that cab. Niggas ain't shit," the woman said as Shy waited.

When the receptionist came back on the line, she told Shy that Freeze was on the West Side Highway and would be there in ten minutes. Shy thanked her and handed the woman back her phone. "Thanks for lettin' me use your phone. My ride should be here in ten minutes."

"No problem, honey. Like I said, I know how niggas get when you don't give them what they want. They buy you a drink or take you to dinner, and they think that's supposed to make us throw our legs open. I think not!"

"Tell me all about it." Shy smiled and sat down next to the woman.

It wasn't long before Shy heard her name called and she saw Freeze waving to her from his truck. Shy thanked the woman for waiting with her and walked toward the truck, knowing that she was safe now.

Chapter Thirty-seven

Mike opened the door for Shy, and she practically fell out of the truck and into his arms. As tears rolled down her cheeks, he kissed her. "Are you all right?" Mike asked with his lips still close to hers.

"I'm fine now." Shy kissed his lips again. "I thought I'd never see you again."

"Did they hurt you?"

"No, they didn't hurt me. They kept me blindfolded and tied to a bed for a while. Then they moved me to a room with a TV and a shower."

Mike looked at his watch. "You have any idea where they were holding you?"

"No. Like I said, I was blindfolded the whole time," Shy told him.

"Hello, Shy. I'm glad you're okay," Bobby said.

Mike turned around. "Bobby," he yelled, "go straight home."

"Yes, Daddy," Bobby said as he walked away laughing.

Mike hailed a cab. "Marriott on Ditmars Boulevard," Mike told the driver.

"By LaGuardia?" the driver asked.

"Yeah," Mike said and avoided making eye contact with Shy. There was a part of him that wanted Shy on the first plane out of New York in the morning.

"Marriott, huh? By the airport, huh?" Shy said and moved closer to Mike in the cab.

"Yeah, it's a nice place and it's close by," he said and put his arm around her. But then there was a part of him that never wanted her out of his sight. He wanted Shy to be happy, and if she would be happy in New York then he would have it make it happen.

"You're sending me back, aren't you?" Shy asked with her head on his chest.

"Oh, I don't know," Mike said, feeling the warmth of her body against his. "You be real nice to me at the Marriott and I might let you stay a few days."

"Hmm," Shy purred. "That sounds so good, baby. I promise to be really, really extra nice to you, 'cause I don't wanna go back," she said, knowing that Mike didn't wanna hear that. But she was home now, and she wanted to stay.

"I know," Mike said and kissed her on the forehead. "But let's not talk about that now. Right now, I'm just happy you're all right, and that you're here with me."

They made love as soon as they got to the hotel, and then drifted off to sleep. Mike didn't stay in bed long. He spent most of the night at the window, thinking. Having Shy back was only part of it. He still had Diego and the DEA to deal with.

PAYBACK

He turned her loose for a reason, Mike thought as he tried to figure out Diego's next move. He got back in the bed and Shy immediately moved closer to him. He put his arm around her.

When Mike woke up, it was a little after noon. Shy was already up and dressed.

"Hi," Shy said, flipping channels on the edge of the bed.

"How you doin'?"

"I'm fine. Glad you finally got some sleep."

"How do you know I hadn't slept?"

"I can always tell when you're not in the bed with me."

"How?"

"I just can." Shy smiled and turned off the TV. "Are you taking me back today?"

"No. You can stay for a while, at least until we work out everything that's been goin' on while you've been laying around at cheap hotels watching TV."

"What been goin' on?" Shy asked.

Mike took his time and broke it all down for her, from Nick in South America to her being kidnapped to Senator Marshall to Diego and those papers. When he was done, Shy said, "Wow. I know that you have a lot to do, so what's on your agenda for today?"

Mike sat up in the bed. "Shopping."

"But you hate to shop."

Once Mike was ready, they went downstairs and caught a cab to Macy's on 34th Street. Along the way, Mike explained that they were going to see Angelo, but he wanted to stop a few times, just in case someone was following them.

"By the way," Shy said. "How long was I gone?"

"Four days."

216

a story by roy glenn

"Four days. Oh yes, I really do need something else to wear."

Since Shy knew how much Mike hated shopping, and because they had things to do, she agreed to get one outfit and come back for more clothes some other time. When they got to Macy's, Mike grabbed a pair of black pants and a shirt. Shy bought a Calvin Klein striped blazer and cropped pant, and a pair of Kimel Efik slide shoes, then they were out of there. On the way out, Shy threw her old clothes in the garbage.

"I've had those clothes on for four days. I don't ever want to see them again. I don't need anything to remind me of that experience." Mike kept his old clothes.

After leaving Macy's, Mike and Shy caught another cab to Harlem. Along the way, Shy looked out the window, enjoying the ride through the city, and thinking about turning herself in and serving her time. Now that she was finally back in New York, she found it was a lot easier to sit in her own island paradise and talk about going to jail. Being in the city was forcing her to realize that she didn't want to do time at all.

When they got to 125th Street and Malcolm X Boulevard, they exited the cab and lost themselves in a sea of people. They didn't buy anything. Mike thought that if anyone was following them, they would be easier to spot. Half an hour later, they were back in a cab and heading uptown through the Bronx on their way to Yonkers.

It was late afternoon when they got to Angelo's place, and to Mike's surprise, Angelo was sitting outside. "Angelo hates the sun." Mike got out of the cab and extended his hand for Shy.

PAYBACK

Angelo stood up. "Mr. *and* Mrs. Black, this is definitely my lucky day. Jimmy, was I just sayin' I feel lucky?"

"Yeah, you was just sayin'," Jimmy agreed.

"Shy," Angelo said and hugged her. "It's good to see you're all right. They didn't hurt you or nothing?"

"No, Angelo, I'm fine. And thank you for helpin' out. I really do appreciate it."

"Forget about it. Anything you need, ever, I'm here for you, the both of you. Now, have a sit-down, and let's enjoy this beautiful, hot-ass day."

"What's up with that anyway? You hate being out in the sun," Mike said.

"I thought, you know, I could sit out here, maybe I could work on my tan or whatever. But the truth is, Mikey, you got your problems, I got mine. Better we talk out here, if you know what I mean."

"I may have those same kind of problems, but I'm sure we'll talk more about that at another time," Mike said.

"To be sure. You still a Yankee fan?" Angelo asked.

"'Til they bury me."

"Let's go to a game while you're here."

"A night game."

"Of course. Hey, we could sit out in the bleachers like we used to when we was comin' up," Angelo said and turned to Shy. "Me and this guy, we used to go to the stadium, drink all the beer we wanted, get drunk, watch a ball game. Those were good times, huh, Mikey?"

"Life was good then, Angee. Look at us now, both of us businessmen with problems."

"Nothing we can't handle."

"That's why I came to see you." Mike leaned close to Angelo and spoke softly. "What can you tell me about this five mill that Diego is here for?"

Angelo looked at Mike for a second then he smiled. "That why I love you, Mikey," he said and then said softly, "You know Diego owns a pharmaceutical company? Frontier Pharmaceuticals is what it's called. But in addition to their legit business, they also manufacture all kinds of other drugs. You know, like Valium, Viagra, Prozac, Paxil, Xanax, shit like that. Well, the way I get it is that he's got a deal with some people from one of the old Soviet republics, Lithuania or someplace like that. Anyway, the deal gets done in a couple of days. Now, let me ask you something."

"What's that?"

"Why you wanna know?"

"I think five million dollars will make this right."

"You gotta love this guy, but it ain't gonna happen. What, you think you was gonna walk in there, take their money and walk out with it?"

"Something like that," Mike said confidently. "Unless you got some reason why I can't."

"It ain't gonna happen, 'cause there's no money to walk out with. The five million gets transferred from one account to the other. It's all done with computers, gives it an air of being a legit transaction."

Mike sat back and thought for a second. "How's Gomez? He still live in the same place?"

PAYBACK

Chapter Thirty-eight

It was a little after 7:00 when Nick parked his car on 74th Street and walked up to Amsterdam Avenue. When he got to Citrus, he noticed a limo parked in front, and a man he thought he recognized was getting in the back seat. Nick remembered the place from the old days. The last time he and Mike were there, they threw somebody through the restaurant's front window.

Mike and Shy were seated at table in the back. When he saw Nick come in, Mike stood up and motioned for him to join them.

"Hello, Shy. It's good to see that you're all right."

"Thank you, Nick. I'm just glad it's over. You look nice," Shy said of Nick, who was dressed in a tuxedo.

"Thank you, Shy," Nick replied graciously as he sat down. "Wasn't that Gomez I saw gettin' in that limo?"

Mike looked at Shy and smiled. "Was it? I didn't see him."

"Must not have been him. You couldn't miss him in a place this size."

"Guess not," Mike said.

a story by roy glenn

"Where you goin', Nick?" Shy asked.

"I'm goin' to meet Wanda. We're goin' to a party at Martin Marshall's house."

"What are you gonna do? Walk up to him and ask if he had a reporter killed?" Mike asked.

"Something like that."

"Handle your business," Shy said.

"How's your partner, Monika?" Mike asked.

"She's doin' a lot better. She's coming with us tonight. We're gonna set up a little something on Marshall tonight," Nick said as Travis, Jackie and Vonda walked in the restaurant.

Mike stood up. "Hello, Jackie," he said and gave her a hug and a kiss on the cheek. Shy rolled her eyes and Jackie returned the favor by rolling her eyes right back at her. "Travis," Mike said and extended his hand. "It's good to finally meet you."

Travis accepted his hand. "Good to meet you too, Mr. Black."

"Black will do. This is my wife, Cassandra. Travis Burns and Jackie Washington."

"Please call me Shy," she said.

Mike turned to Nick. "Have you two met?" he asked and pointed at Travis.

"No," Nick told him. "Nick Simmons." The two shook hands.

"I know you gotta go, Nick." Mike paused. "Why don't you take Travis with you tonight? From what I hear, Mr. Burns is very good with computers. He might be useful."

"Yeah," Nick said nodding his head. "I think we can find some use for him tonight." Nick turned to Travis. "You ready?"

PAYBACK

"Yes," Travis said and followed Nick out the door. He was excited just to be invited to meet Mike Black, and to have him say that he might be useful made his night.

"Don't worry, Jackie. Nick will take good care of your boy."

"Travis is a big boy. He can take care of himself," Jackie said and sat down.

"Who are you?" Mike asked as Vonda was about to take a seat.

"Black, this is Vonda. She's the new member of our team."

"It's good to meet you, Vonda, but why don't you wait over there?" Mike said and pointed at the bar.

While Vonda walked toward the bar, Mike asked Jackie, "Can I order you something?" He signaled for a waiter.

Jackie picked up a menu. "I'll have Hennessy on the rocks and some shrimp dumplings," she told the waiter.

"And the lady at bar," Mike said to the waiter and pointed at Vonda. "Put whatever she orders on my check." Once the waiter was gone, Mike said, "I heard that you were very valuable to Freeze the other night."

"I just did what I had to do," Jackie replied.

"I appreciate that," Mike said and discreetly handed her an envelope. "I won't forget what you did."

"Thank you." Jackie put the envelope in her purse.

"I may have some other things that you could do for me." Jackie's mind wandered to the things she'd like to do for him. "But we'll talk about that some other time," Mike said and turned to Shy.

"You used to work at Frontier Pharmaceuticals, right?" Shy asked.

a story by roy glenn

"I sure did. I used to be a chemist, until they fired me for insubordination for refusing to work on a project on my own time."

"That's not right," Shy said. "What I need, Jackie, is for you to tell me everything you know about Frontier."

While Jackie sipped on Hennessy and munched on her shrimp dumplings steamed in a jalapeno sauce, she told Shy what she wanted to know. Once Jackie was finished, Shy told her exactly what she wanted her to do.

PAYBACK

Chapter Thirty-nine

At the home of Senator Martin Marshall, the party had begun. The house was packed to overflowing with his guests, talking, drinking, and snacking on finger food. Marshall's guests were the rich and powerful—the political crowd, for the most part, a few wealthy campaign contributors, and the usual array of hangers-on who always seemed to show up at these types of events.

Earlier in the evening, when Nick and Travis picked up Monika, she came out of the house dressed in a beautiful electric blue silk gown by Stephen Yearick. It had a straight neckline, multiple beaded straps over the left shoulder, a low asymmetrical back, and asymmetrical beading in silver and midnight blue. She had wrapped her head with a scarf that matched her dress to cover her bandages, and a patch over her eye. The sight of her walking toward the car caused Nick to laugh as she struggled to walk in heels. Travis sat up straight in his seat and took notice of her hips swaying from side to side. "Only for you, Nick," Monika said as she got in the car. "And not a word about these heels. I don't know how I ever got anywhere in these things."

After Nick filled Monika in on the details of the job they were going to run, they went and picked up their surveillance van. While Monika gave Travis a crash course on the equipment and what he had to do, Nick caught a cab to pick up Wanda and Glynnis.

Once they were inside, Glynnis drifted off to socialize with her colleagues, leaving Nick and Wanda alone. Wanda looked at Nick. "You look very nice in a tux, Nick."

"I was just about to tell you how beautiful you look tonight, but you always look beautiful."

"Well, thank you, Nick." Wanda blushed. She wore a black crepe gown with a sweetheart neckline with beaded straps from center bust and sheer insets at the waist. "I thought you were going to bring someone else with you. I was hoping to meet her."

"She's here. I saw her wandering around when we first got here. I didn't want us to be seen together. You'll meet her soon enough. She's checkin' out the house to get the layout in case we need to come back again. In fact, do you see that woman over there with the blue dress?"

"The one with the patch over her eye?"

"That's her," Nick said.

"She pretty, Nick."

"You're not jealous, are you, Wanda?" Nick hoped.

"No, of course not. Why should I be jealous?"

"Why should you?"

Truth be told, Wanda was beginning to enjoy Nick's company and was just a bit jealous, but she wasn't ready to admit it, not even to herself, so she changed the subject. "Have you spotted Marshall yet?"

"No, not yet," Nick replied and looked around the room. "But he's here somewhere, I don't think he'd miss his own party."

While Wanda and Nick waited for Marshall to show himself, Travis sat outside in the van. It was like being a kid on Christmas morning, as Travis played with all of the devices Monika had introduced him to. His assignment in this operation was to watch and listen. Monika explained that the image on screen before him was a satellite-generated, 3-dimensional thermal image of Marshall's house. She told him that the red lines represented walls, so he could see each room in the house.

"What are those dots in each room?" Travis had asked earlier.

"Those represent everybody in the house. But we're not gonna use that this time," Monika said and turned that function off. "Once we get inside, you'll see two moving indicators. One will be me, and the other will be Nick. Are you familiar with the Greek alphabet?"

"Yes."

"Nick is Alpha, I'm Beta and you are Omega. Once we identify Marshall, I'll tag him and you'll be able to track him too. He'll be Gamma."

The other device that Monika had Travis monitor and was a parabolic microphone, which magnified distant sounds, allowing him to locate the source of sound and suppress background noises. "Because of its special design, it is capable of picking up and magnifying signals up to seventy-five times that of a normal omni-directional microphone," Monika told him.

While he waited for Monika to tag Marshall, Travis was amusing himself by listening to different sounds and conversations going on around the house. He listened to a couple of boring conversations at the party, picked up and identified where the kitchen and the bathroom were, and even overheard a couple having sex in one of the rooms on the second floor.

Travis was drifting from conversation to conversation when he found one that interested him. He knew he had something when he heard Black's name mentioned, and immediately began recording the conversation.

" . . . I don't want there to be any way this can come back and bite me."

"You worry too much, my friend. Once the word begins to spread about his involvement in this business, his political allies will run for cover and you will have no need to fear him."

"But if you can't find that *package* or whatever you call it, and it becomes public, it will put me and a lot of our friends in an extremely compromised position."

"If that happens, which it won't, because I assure you that the package will be recovered, we have set these things in motion so the spotlight will be on Mike Black and—" the man laughed, "and others that I will make known to you when the time is right."

"There is one other thing that concerns me."

"What is that, my friend?"

"DeFrancisco. He's shaky. I am not sure we can trust him to keep his mouth shut if anything goes wrong."

PAYBACK

"How much does he really know? What have you told him?"

"I only told him what he needed to know to put the operation in motion. Still, he has me, and I don't need any more heat. I just got somebody else's stink off me."

"He is your man. When he has outlived his usefulness, you will have to insure his silence."

"I've got to get back downstairs."

"I understand completely. I will leave through the service entrance."

After that, Travis heard footsteps and the door opening and closing. He tried to follow the walking sound, but he couldn't stay with it.

"This is Beta," Monika said into her wireless microphone. "Objective acquired. I'm moving toward him."

"Acknowledged," Nick said.

"Acknowledged, Beta. I have you," Travis said, feeling like old times.

Monika began to approach Marshall, who was standing with two women and a man. She grabbed a glass of champagne from a waiter as he passed and stood close to Marshall. When he turned to walk away, Monika stepped in his path and purposely bumped into him. She placed a very small device on the sleeve of his jacket. Marshall smiled when he saw Monika. "I am terribly sorry, Miss . . ."

"Ryan, Jeri Ryan," Monika said.

"Martin Marshall."

"I know who you are, and it's a pleasure to meet you. And it's me who owes you an apology. I should watch where I'm going. A bit too much champagne," Monika said and raised her glass.

"Are you okay? Do you need somebody to drive you home?" Marshall looked at Monika the way a predator looks at his prey, and took a step closer.

"No, I'm sure I'll be fine," Monika said and tried to move away from him.

"Are you sure?"

"Yes, I'm quite sure, but thank you for the offer."

"I hope you don't mind me asking, but I was wondering about the eye patch."

"I was hurt in an accident recently. They weren't able to save the eye."

"Oh, I'm sorry to hear that. Are you all right?"

"Other than this, I'm fine," Monika said, anxious to get away from Marshall. "Well, Mr. Marshall, it was a pleasure meeting you."

"And you as well, Ms. Ryan." Marshall handed her a card. "Call me sometime. Maybe we can get together and have a drink."

"I'm sure that pretty wife of yours won't like that at all," Monika said and walked away. When she had gotten far enough away, she said, "Objective is tagged."

"Acknowledged, Beta. Omega, do you have him?"

"I have him, Alpha," Travis said.

"Acknowledged, Omega. I'm coming to you," Monika said and began moving toward the front door.

"Advise me when you get there, Beta," Nick said.

"Acknowledged."

"What happens now?" Wanda asked.

"We wait until Monika gets back to the truck and then we'll make our move," Nick told her.

"I just gotta say, this is all very exciting to me."

Nick smiled. "What's that, Wanda?"

PAYBACK

"All this spy stuff. You know I don't get out much, so like I said, I'm just glad to be a part of it all. Did Mike say anything when you told him I was coming with you?"

"No. He knows it's you that has the contacts. What could he say?"

"Do the words *conspiracy to commit a felony* mean anything to you, Wanda?" she said, trying to sound like Mike.

"You're right." Nick laughed. Mike had always been very protective about what parts of the business he involved Wanda in. "Maybe it won't be an issue for much longer."

"Maybe."

"You think we're really gettin' out?"

"I don't know, Nick," Wanda said and looked into his eyes. She had the strongest urge to kiss him, but she ignored it. "We'll just have to wait and see."

"This is Beta. I'm in position," Monika said when she got to the van.

"Acknowledged, Beta. Assume operational control."

"Acknowledged."

Travis started to get up.

"Where do you think you're goin'?" Monika asked.

"I thought that meant he wanted you in this spot," Travis said, looking confused.

"I am assuming operational control. I am now in command here. That's what that means to me." Monika looked around the van. "This is your baby, you handle it. I blow shit up." And with that, Travis sat down.

"I got something I want you and Nick to listen to later. I recorded it earlier. I think it might be important."

a story by roy glenn

Back inside the Marshall house, Nick got ready to make his move. He asked Wanda if she would get Glynnis to walk him over and introduce him to Marshall. "I can introduce you to him," Wanda said. "I mean, I do know him."

"I'm sure that you do," Nick said as they walked. "But if he knows you, then he knows that you work for Mike Black, and I want to keep him out of it."

Wanda looked at Nick skeptically. "Okay. As long as you're not just trying to protect me. I'm a big girl, you know."

Nick's eyes traveled over Wanda's body. "I can see that."

Wanda smiled. "I can take care of myself," she said as they found Glynnis.

"So, you guys ready to meet the man?" Glynnis asked.

"He is, I'm not," Wanda said. "Nick is afraid that Marshall will connect me to Mike. "

"Yes, that's right. I didn't think of that."

"Neither did I." Wanda frowned. "So, I'm going home. Will you be all right, Glynnis?"

"Oh sure, Wanda. I'll be fine with this crowd."

"Okay, then. Will you *please* call me later, Nick?" She looked at Glynnis. "Just to let me know how things worked out?"

"I promise I'll call you later."

Chapter Forty

Nick and Glynnis watched Wanda until she was out of the house. Glynnis turned to Nick. "Okay, handsome, let's go."

"When we get to him, Glynnis, introduce me as Patrick Mitchell."

"Patrick Mitchell, right."

When Nick and Glynnis approached Marshall, he was talking to two men. "Hello, Martin," Glynnis said and tapped him on the shoulder.

Marshall turned around. "Glynnis, it's so good to see you," he said and turned to the men he was with. "Will you gentlemen excuse me?" he asked.

"I'll give you a call, Marty. We can discuss this further over eighteen holes," one of the men said.

"I'll make some time on my schedule," Marshall promised and the men went away. "Thank you for coming to my rescue, Glynnis. Lobbyists always want something."

a story by roy glenn

"I know how that goes, believe me. I want to introduce you to Patrick Mitchell. Patrick, this is Martin Marshall. He's a state senator."

"Patrick, right? Good to meet you."

"It's an honor to meet you, sir," Nick said and the two shook hands.

"Oh," Glynnis said. "There goes Chris. I just have to talk to him. I'll be right back, Patrick." Glynnis hurried away, leaving Nick alone with Marshall.

"So, what business are you in, Patrick? Don't tell me that you're a lobbyist," Marshall joked.

"No, sir, nothing as complicated as that. I'm a private investigator."

"Really?" Marshall said and laughed a little. "What are you investigating? And please don't say your investigating me."

"Actually, I wanted to talk to you about a murder."

"A murder?"

"Tavia Hawkins. Do you know her?" Nick asked, and Marshall's facial expression changed.

"I'm afraid I do. That woman has made a career of writing lies about me. Did she send you?"

"No, sir. She was found dead last night."

"Oh my goodness, that's terrible. How did it happen?"

"An overdose of sleeping pills."

"Sleeping pills? I thought you said she was murdered."

"I never actually said she was murdered. I just asked if you know her."

"I see. How can I help you, Mr. Mitchell?"

PAYBACK

"I know the story she was working on was about you," Nick lied. "I was wondering what you could tell me about that."

"I have no idea what you're talking about." Marshall smiled. "But I'd be happy to do what I can to help. Let's get together and talk about this at another time." Marshall handed Nick his card. "Call me at my office and I'll look into it. Now, if you'll excuse me."

"Yes, of course. You have guests to attend to and I'm monopolizing your time. I'll give you a call tomorrow and we can talk more then." Nick extended his hand. "Once again, it was an honor meeting you, sir."

"You as well. I'll look forward to your call." Marshall watched Nick until he lost sight of him. He looked around the room again and began walking very quickly through the crowd. Marshall approached a man talking to a group of ladies.

"Excuse me for interrupting, ladies. Scotty, can I speak with you in my office? I promise it will only take a minute, ladies, and then you can have him back."

Marshall and Scotty made their way through the crowd to Marshall's office. By that time, Nick was in the van with Monika and Travis. Marshall entered the office and slammed the door. "I thought you were gonna take care of Hawkins."

"I did," Scotty answered with a blank expression on his face. "I did just like you told me. Made it look like she OD'ed on sleeping pills."

"Right. Then maybe you can tell me why I just got finished talking to some private detective about her."

"What?"

"You heard me. He said he wanted to talk to me about a murder, not a suicide, Scotty, a murder!" Marshall yelled. "He was here, in my house."

"I'm sure that the police ruled her death a suicide. I checked with my source."

"Then it would make sense that the only way he could connect her to me is the evidence."

"Marty, I took care of that. I shredded the paper trail and wiped her files from her work and home computers. I even took any disks she had laying around."

"Then why was he here? Are you sure you didn't leave anything on her computer?"

"I'm sure. The program I use is called Evidence-Eliminator. It eliminates the specific application files, temp files, system backups. It even wipes Outlook's deleted items and sent items. And when it's done, it eliminates the program. You know I've used it to clean up hundreds of times and it's never failed me before."

"Then why was he here?" Marshall asked softly this time.

"I don't know," Scotty answered in the same tone.

"Then you better find out."

"What's his name?"

"Patrick Mitchell. He's going to call me tomorrow. You get on top of this, find out what he knows and who he's told, and do it quick."

"I understand."

"And don't mention any of this to DeFrancisco. He's an idiot and he talks too much."

Outside in the van, Monika laughed. "Yeah, asshole, you talk too much too. Got your ass on tape."

PAYBACK

"Nick," Travis said, "I was tellin' Monika that I got something I recorded earlier that I think you need to hear."

"What's that, Travis?"

"It's a recording of two men talkin'. I knew it was important when they started talkin' about Black. And now I'm sure one of the voices was Marshall's."

Travis played the recording back for Nick and Monika. After listening, Nick agreed that it was Marshall's voice.

"But who's the other guy?" Monika asked.

"Diego Estabon."

Chapter Forty-one

Diego entered his hotel suite and immediately poured himself a glass of Tequila. Although there was a woman lying on the bed, he didn't speak to her. Diego walked to the window and looked out. As he looked out at the Manhattan skyline, he thought about how well things were progressing for him. Tomorrow he would make an easy five million dollars on the sale of prescription drugs, and there would be more to come.

Diego had to laugh at his good fortune. He had bought the failing pharmaceutical company years ago as a way to launder his drug profits. It was only recently that he started selling prescription drugs over the Internet, never expecting that there would come a day when he would be able to make this kind of money. And if the buyers were the serious businessmen they claimed to be, then this would be just the first of many more such deals.

PAYBACK

DeFrancisco had gone to great lengths to assure him that the DEA investigation of Black was moving into the next phase.

Even though he had assured Marshall that the papers would be recovered, Diego was still very concerned that they would become public. Those papers contained detailed information about his drug operation. Although he never told anybody, those papers came into existence because of his carelessness.

Her name was Isabelle, or at least that's what she called herself. She was young and beautiful, and for a time, Diego lost himself in her. Over a three-year period, Isabelle worked her way into Diego's bed and into his confidence. In reality, Isabelle was a deep cover operative for the DEA. It was only by chance that he found her out when DeFrancisco told him that he had gotten wind of a South American operation and mentioned details that he'd heard. Diego knew the only person who could have that type of information was Isabelle.

It hurt him deeply to do it, but he killed her. Still, it was too late. Isabelle had completed and filed a report, and had turned the papers over to her control, whom she met in Singapore when she and Diego visited there. Diego had him murdered as well, and had made arrangements to recover the report, but things went wrong, and the papers got into the open. To this date, they still had not been recovered. He knew that if those papers became public, his associates would be indicted. If that happened, they would surely kill them.

His plan was simple: divert as much attention away from himself and his operation by giving the DEA some other high-profile target. He would make it appear that Black had ordered the murders of Chilly, Felix and the General, and would soon murder D-Train and take over the drug traffic.

Diego never forgot that Black caused him to go to jail. He had never gotten over the shame he suffered when Black and Bobby came out of the club. They laughed when they saw him in handcuffs with his face pressed against the hood of his car. So, setting Black up to take the fall with the DEA would serve two purposes. It would keep Diego and his associates out of the spotlight, and it would be payback for the humiliation Diego suffered because of Black.

There was one other person that he had not forgiven for past humiliation. That was his father, Gomez.

"Diego," the woman said to him, "aren't you going to at least say hello to me?"

"Hello, Esperanza," Diego said without looking at her.

"Aren't you glad to see me?" Esperanza asked.

"Overjoyed, my love," he replied and continued to stare out the window.

"Have I done something to displease you?"

"No, my love, everything is fine. Now, stop asking me questions."

Esperanza got up from the bed and walked toward Diego. She stood behind him and put her arms around his waist. "I thought that you were going to take me to dinner, Diego."

"We are still going."

Esperanza moved to Diego's side. "Don't you like the way I am dressed, Diego?"

PAYBACK

"You look lovely," Diego told her, but still hadn't looked in her direction.

"I knew it," Esperanza said angrily. "You don't like it."

"I did not say that."

"You didn't have to. I can tell by the way you said it. You hate it."

"I did not say that, Esperanza. I said that you look lovely. Like a goddess."

"You lie, Diego. So, I will take it off," Esperanza said and walked away from Diego, undressing. He turned to watch her. "This is how you like me to dress, isn't it, Diego? You love to see me naked, don't you, Diego?" She lay across the bed.

"Yes, my love. I love you when you are naked," he said and his cell phone rang. Diego took a deep breath and looked at Esperanza, who had begun to play with herself for his amusement. "Excuse me, my love," he said and answered the phone. "Hello."

"Diego Estabon."

"Yes, who is this?"

"We have your father," the digitally disguised voice said. "And if you ever want to see him alive again, you will do exactly what we tell you. Any deviation from our instructions will cause your father great pain before he dies."

"Who is this?" Diego demanded to know.

"Who I am is not important. Who we have is."

"What do you want?"

"You have two days to get five million dollars. Have the money ready by eight o'clock. You'll receive further instructions."

"I want to talk to my father right now," Diego insisted.

240

"Diego," Gomez said to his son. "Do what these people say, Diego, and give them what they ask."

"Remember, five million dollars in two days or your father dies," the digital voice said and disconnected the line.

Diego hung up the phone and immediately called his father's house and his cell phone, but got no answer. There were at least five men at Gomez's house at all times. Had the kidnappers killed them all and took Gomez?

"Is everything all right?" Esperanza asked.

"Shut up." Diego went to the door and opened it. Three of his men were sitting outside. "I want you to go to my father's house and call me when you get there."

"Yes, Papi," the man said and left.

Diego closed the door. *This can't be happening.* He sat down on the bed and buried his head in his hands.

"What is wrong, Diego?" Esperanza asked and put her hand on his shoulder. Diego pushed her away.

"I told you to shut up or get out."

"But, Diego, I just want to help."

Diego quickly got up from the bed and grabbed her dress from the floor. Then he returned to the bed and grabbed Esperanza by the hand. Diego dragged her to the door, opened it, threw the dress into the hall, and Esperanza behind it.

Diego slammed the door and returned to the bed. He needed Gomez alive if his plan was to work. It wouldn't be enough to hand them Mike Black. When Black was arrested for those drug-related murders and they started looking for a supplier, Diego would hand them Gomez and he would disappear.

PAYBACK

He had never forgiven Gomez for not doing enough to get him out of jail and out of the country after the incident with Black. "You need to be taught a lesson to not involve yourself in matters that don't concern you." He could still hear Gomez saying this to him at the time. "Maybe jail will make a man of you," Gomez told him. He had always hated Gomez for treating him like a child. No matter what he did, it would never measure up to Gomez.

In the end, Gomez did get his case heard before a sympathetic judge, got the drug charge thrown out and provided him protection, even status while he was in prison. Still, Diego swore that he would pay him back.

If this had happened at any other time, he might have told the kidnappers to kill Gomez then hung up the phone, but not now. Now he needed Gomez alive.

Chapter Forty-two

Melinda parked her car outside of Cuisine and turned off the engine. She sat there for a moment thinking about how everything had gone wrong.

How could things have gotten so fucked up? Melinda asked herself. The answer was simple. *Maybe you're not as smart as you think you are.*

Melinda thought she had D-Train wrapped around her little finger. She felt the stinging in her cheek and knew that wasn't true. Melinda got out of the car and went inside.

I'ma make damn sure his ass pays for that.

Not much had changed at Cuisine since the last time she was there. Same band, still playing the same music. Melinda thought back to all the times when she would walk in the club with Black and the band would break into "The Girl from Ipanema." She wondered aloud if that was still his favorite song.

Melinda took a seat at the bar, knowing that it would be a waste of time to ask for Freeze. Everybody would just act like they never heard of him. Melinda looked around for somebody that she knew, but there were a lot of new faces. The bartender came and asked her what she was drinking.

"Double Black Russian."

When the bartender returned with her drink, Melinda sipped and enjoyed the show while she continued to look for somebody she knew or for Freeze to come out of the office. She looked at the door to the office and the man standing by it. Maybe she could use her charm to get him to let her back there, but she knew better. That's when she saw a familiar face coming toward her. Melinda couldn't remember her name. All she remembered was that she used to fuck Freeze.

As the woman got closer, she smiled. "Melinda?"

"Hi," Melinda said faking surprise.

"How are you doin"? I haven't seen you in a long time."

"Yeah, I haven't been here in years," Melinda said casually. "I'm sorry, but I don't remember your name."

"Alexia."

"That's right, Alexia. I see a lot of new faces, but other than that, not much has changed."

"Well, there have been a few changes since you were here last, but you're right, not much has changed."

"I heard Freeze is running the place now."

"He sure does."

"Is he here? I'd love to say hello."

"He was in the office. If he's still here, I'll let him know that you want to holla at him," Alexia said.

"Don't go to any trouble. It ain't that deep," Melinda lied.

"It's no trouble at all," Alexia said, tired of making small talk. She couldn't stand Melinda when she used to come to the club.

Always thought she was better than everybody just 'cause she was fuckin' Black, she thought as she walked off.

By the time Melinda finished her drink, Alexia was back. "Come with me," she told Melinda and started walking toward the office. When they got to the door that led to the office, security handed Alexia a metal detecting wand, then he took Melinda's purse and searched it. When they were both satisfied that Melinda wasn't carrying a gun, Alexia escorted her to Freeze.

Alexia opened the door and showed Melinda in. There sat Freeze at what she remembered as Black's desk. A rush of memories washed over her, and Melinda saw herself lying on that desk, having the most fantastic sex. Only now, there was a gun lying where she used to lay. "Hello, Freeze."

"What's up?" Freeze tilted his head to the side. "What happened to your face? Your boy Curl do that to you?"

"It's nothing. It's what I got for thinking I was smart, that's all, No big deal, Freeze."

"So, what are you doin' here? I know you didn't come here trying to get me to do something about that. So, what's up?"

"I came here to tell you what you wanna know."

"What do I wanna know?"

"Who killed Pauleen and why."

"I'm listening."

"A guy named Paul Clay, they call him Clark Kent."

PAYBACK

"Yeah, but he's dead, so tell me something I don't know. Who killed him?"

"D-Train killed him."

"Stop fuckin' around and tell me why," Freeze demanded.

"Because he missed you and killed Pauleen instead. He wants you dead so he can get to Black. But he knew Black wouldn't talk to him; he'd have to go through you. And besides, Black been busy trying to find his bitch."

"How you know about that?"

"It ain't no secret. Black and Bobby been ridin' all over the city lookin' for that bitch, and they haven't exactly been nice and quiet about it. Word gets around quick."

"So, why does he want to get to Black?"

"He doesn't think that you're on his level, so he needs Black to sit down with him, like he did with Chilly. You see, after your boy killed Chilly, D and two of his people wanna step up to Chilly's position in the game."

"You mean them other niggas don't respect him."

"Yup."

"Figures. I always thought Curl was a bitch and Chilly was fuckin' him."

Melinda had no comment.

"Oh, I'm sorry. I'm talkin' about the man you love. But now that he slapped the shit outta your pretty ass, you come sneakin' back here wantin' me to do something about it."

Melinda dropped her head and said quietly, "Yes."

Freeze laughed. "That's okay, Melinda."

"You get what you want, I get what I want. It's business. It's just business for personal reasons."

a story by roy glenn

"Where is he?"

"I know where he'll be in about an hour."

Nick turned corner and drove slowly down Wanda's block. He promised that he would call to let her know what happened with Marshall, but decided to drop by instead. *This might prove to be a bit more interesting,* Nick thought as he got closer to Wanda's house. He figured by now she had come out of that evening gown that she looked so good in, and had changed into that robe she had on the night they talked. Since he saw no lines, Nick wondered if Wanda had anything on under it. Maybe tonight he would find out.

He put the car in park and was about to get out when his cell rang. He started to ignore it, but quickly thought about the last time he ignored a call and what happened to Monika because of it. He looked at the display. It was Freeze. "What's up?"

"I need you to ride with me," Freeze said.

"Now?"

"Yeah, now."

"Okay," Nick said and started the car. "Where are you?"

"I'm at Cuisine. Where you at?" Freeze asked. "I'll come get you."

"No," Nick said quickly. "I'm on my way to you."

Freeze laughed. "I'll see you when you get here."

When Nick got to Cuisine, Freeze was standing outside by his truck waiting for him. Nick got out of his car, got his bag out of the trunk and came toward Freeze, who started walking away. When Nick caught up with him, Freeze pointed to the cars parked along the street. "Pick one. Make it a four-door."

PAYBACK

Nick knew they were going to ride on somebody. The only question was who? Nick looked around and walked toward a '95 Lincoln.

"What did you find out?" Nick asked.

"I'll tell you on the way," Freeze said and took out a Slim Jim and unlocked the car door. After disabling the alarm, Freeze quickly hotwired the car and they were on their way.

When they arrived at Melinda's condo, Freeze picked out a dark spot to park. He got in the back seat and they waited for D-Train to show up. Nick reached in his bag and pulled out his night vision goggles.

Freeze began to laugh as Nick put them on. "Are those really necessary?"

"Yes, they are. You wanna try them?"

"Yeah, let me see them." Freeze took the goggles from Nick and put them on. "Hey," he paused and looked around. "These shits ain't bad. I can see every fuckin' thing." Freeze took them off and handed them back to Nick. "You gotta get me some of those."

"I knew a killa like you would like something like these. Make you a more efficient killa."

While they waited, Freeze gave some thought to the fact that he was waiting to get revenge over the killing of a woman who cheated on him. But that didn't really matter. Like he told Melinda, it was business, it was just business for personal reasons. D-Train needed to go, if for no other reason than to make an example of him. Killing D-Train would keep the others in check. It would solidify his position. Black earned his position, earned everybody's respect in war. Freeze had been given the position. That's why niggas were willing to try him.

Freeze decided that just riding by blasting wasn't good enough. He had to stand in front of D-Train and look into his eyes when he killed him.

Melinda told him that if he was coming alone, he'd be driving a gold Lexus. If he had a bodyguard with him, they would be in a dark blue Chevy Suburban. It wasn't too much longer before Melinda was proven right.

"Dark blue Chevy Suburban coming this way."

"How many?"

"Two."

"Makes it easy." Freeze waited until they parked and D-Train got out and went inside. "Wait here," Freeze said, put on his gloves and got out. "Yo, let me borrow them things." Nick took off the goggles and gave them to Freeze. "I'll be right back."

The driver of the Suburban rolled down his window, kicked 50-Cent up a little louder and made himself comfortable. Freeze waited ten minutes before he approached the car. Freeze put the silencer on his gun and continued toward the truck. When he got to the window, Freeze pointed his weapon and fired twice, one shot to the head and the other to the chest, then kept walking toward the building.

Melinda explained to Freeze that she told D-Train she might be a little late getting there, so he could let himself in to take a shower and wait for her in bed. D-Train was sorry that he had slapped her, and was anxious to make it up to her. Earlier in the day, he had bought Melinda a diamond-studded necklace. *I know she's gonna love this.* He did as he was told, showered, and got in the bed. He placed the jewelry

PAYBACK

box on the nightstand next to the bed and waited for Melinda to arrive.

Freeze unlocked the door with the key Melinda gave him, then made a few scratch marks on the lock to make it look like forced entry. With Nick's night vision goggles on, Freeze was able to move quickly to the bedroom. Freeze came through the door.

"Time to die, muthafucka." Freeze fired six times, hitting D-Train with all six shots. Then he walked over to him and put one more bullet in his head to make sure he was gone.

As Freeze stood over D-Train's dead body, he noticed the jewelry box on the bed. He opened the box. "Nice." Freeze put the box in his pocket and left the condo.

Chapter Forty-three

It had been a long night. While Nick played spy and Freeze did what he does best, Mike and Shy went dancing at Impressions. Both had called Mike and made him aware of the events of the evening. Mike decided that it was time to let Bobby know what was going on. Mike went upstairs to Bobby's office to make a call.

"What's up?" Bobby answered.

"There're some things that I need to talk to you about."

"I'm listening."

"Not over the phone. Where you at?"

"Where you at?"

"Impressions."

"I'm on my way," Bobby said and hung up the phone.

It took him a while to get there, but he finally got to the office a little after two in the morning. "'Bout time," Mike said and stood up.

Shy stood up too. "Just in time to take us home."

PAYBACK

"Oh, so I'm a taxi cab now, huh?" Bobby laughed and started shuffling toward the door. "Well, sir, ma'am, yous all just come on and go with old Bobby Ray." Bobby stopped. "Bobby Ray, that's me. I'll get yous all home just as fast as these old bones and my new Cadillac can carry us." Mike and Shy both shook their heads and followed Bobby out of the club to his car. On the way to Mike's house, he brought Bobby up to speed on what happened that night.

Then Shy asked a question. "Bobby?"

"Yes, ma'am."

"Would you stop that?" Shy insisted.

"Yes, ma'am—I mean, what you want?"

"Do you mind if I ask you a question?"

"What do you want to know?"

"I know this is none of my business, but I gotta ask you. Are you cheating on Pam?"

Bobby looked at Mike, who shrugged his shoulders and looked out the window.

"I . . . you see, ah . . . it's not . . ." Bobby stuttered.

His cell phone rang.

"Saved by the bell," Mike said and continued looking out the window.

Bobby looked at the display and answered the phone with fury. "I thought I told you that I was busy and I would get with you tomorrow."

"Bobby, it's Pam," she said in a monotone.

Bobby quickly glanced at the display. Pam was calling from Cat's apartment. *This can't be good.*

"What goin' on, Pam?" Bobby asked tentatively.

"I'm at your girlfriend's apartment. Is Mike with you?"

"He's right here. Do you want to talk to him?"

"No, I don't want to talk to Mike. I need the two of you to come here."

"Where is here, Pam?"

"Bobby, don't play with me," Pam said calmly and evenly. "I need you and Mike to come here now," Pam said and hung up the phone.

Bobby dropped his phone and made a U-turn.

"Everything all right, Bobby?" Mike asked.

"Pam is at Cat's apartment."

"I guess that answers my question," Shy said and laughed a little.

Bobby drove as fast as he could to Cat's apartment. When they arrived and went inside the building, none of them were prepared for what they found.

Bobby got to the door, and much to his surprise, it was cracked open. He pushed the door slowly and stepped inside. "Pam . . . Pam, are you here?" The apartment was in darkness, lit only by the streetlights shining through the window.

"I'm right here, Bobby," Pam said as Mike and Shy entered the apartment.

"Where is here, Pam?"

"In the kitchen," she answered.

"Is everything all right?" Bobby asked as he got closer to her. Then he stopped and took a step back. "Gun."

Mike quickly stepped in front of Bobby, which caused Shy's eyes to buck wide open. "What's up with the gun, Pam?"

Pam looked at the weapon in her hand. "It's for killing, Mike. You know better than most people what a gun is for."

PAYBACK

"Are you all right, Pam?" Shy asked, noticing the look on Pam's face and the tone of her voice.

"Hello, Shy. It's good to see you. I hope the kidnappers didn't hurt you."

"No, Pam," Shy said. "I'm fine, but I'm worried about you, sweetie."

"You don't have to worry about me, Shy. Everything is going to be just fine now."

"Why don't you give me the gun, Pam?" Mike asked quietly as he walked toward her with his hand out.

Pam pointed it at Mike. "Here," she said and handed the gun to him. "I'm finished with it."

Now that she was no longer armed, Bobby stepped toward his wife again. "Pam," he said softly. "Are you all right?"

"I'm fine, Bobby."

"Where's Cat?"

"She's in the bedroom."

Bobby and Mike went to the bedroom and opened the door. There on the floor was Cat, with a gunshot wound in the chest. Bobby knelt down next to her and checked for a pulse. "She dead?" Mike asked.

"Yeah." Bobby touched her face then closed her eyes. He felt like somebody had kicked his insides out.

Mike and Bobby came out of the bedroom and went back to the kitchen, where Shy was talking to Pam. "What happened, Pam?" Shy asked.

"She called the house again," Pam began. She may have been talking to Shy, but she was looking at Bobby. It was obvious that Pam was in shock after what she had done. "She said that she had just gotten finished fucking Bobby and he would still be there if Mike hadn't called and asked Bobby to pick him up. I told her that I didn't believe her, so she described

254

everything that Bobby had on, right down to his boxers. Well, we went through the usual *bitch this*, and *ho that*, and then she said that she was going to take Bobby away from me and that our house was going to be their house. I was about to hang up, 'cause I had heard enough of her shit, but she kept on talking. She said 'Yeah, bitch, I been to your muthafuckin' house.' "

"I never brought her to the house," Bobby said in defense of himself.

"He didn't have to, Shy. She came on her own. She said this afternoon when I went to pick up the children from school, she came in the house."

"That's bullshit! How could she get past the alarm?" Bobby yelled.

"That's the same thing I asked her, Shy. She said she knew the code. You see, Bobby talks in his sleep sometimes, and he'll tell you anything you wanna know when he's like that. Well, I guess she knows that too, 'cause she told me that all she did is ask and he gave her the code to the alarm."

Mike and Shy both looked at Bobby. Mike shook his head; Shy rolled her eyes.

"I still didn't believe that she was bold enough to go in our house, so she described every room. She went in the children's rooms. The rooms where our children sleep, Bobby," Pam said, finally addressing him. "She described our bedroom. She told me how I arranged the clothes and shoes in my closet. She even told me what was in my jewelry box. Then she said that our bed was very comfortable, and that she was looking forward to fuckin' Bobby on our bed. That's when I hung up on her.

PAYBACK

"But then I thought about it. This woman is crazy. Crazy enough to come in our house and not only search it, but call and tell me about it. She wasn't gonna stop. I told Bobby to stop her, or I would stop her.

"So I called her back. I told her that we needed to talk face to face. I was surprised when she invited me over. I took the kids to my sister's house and I came here. When I got here, she asked me to follow her. Said she wanted to show me something and led me straight to the bedroom. She opened the door and pointed to the bed. She said this is where her and Bobby fuck every day. That's when I shot her."

Chapter Forty-four

Mike and Bobby looked at one another. "The parlor?" Bobby asked.

"No doubt," Mike replied.

"The parlor?" Shy asked. "What's the parlor?"

"Funeral parlor. We owned it for years. It comes in handy for occasions like this," Mike answered his still confused wife.

"Come on, Mike. You can explain that shit to her later. We need to get Pam and this body outta here," Bobby said and Mike had to agree.

"We'll come back later and clean up this place. Cassandra, take Pam to the car and take her home."

Bobby throw Shy his keys. "Pam, where's your car?"

"At home."

"How did you get here?"

"I took a cab and had the driver drop me off two blocks from here. I walked the rest of the way," Pam said.

PAYBACK

"Okay, just take Pam to the car and wait for us," Mike told Shy.

"Shy, there's an alley that leads to the back of the building. Meet us there," Bobby said and went back in the bedroom.

"Come on, Pam," Shy said and led Pam by the arm out of the apartment.

After Shy left with Pam, Mike followed Bobby into the bedroom. He found Bobby kneeling beside the body.

When he saw Mike come into the room, Bobby stood up. "Damn, I didn't think Pam had it in her to do something like this."

Mike went to the bed and grabbed the bedspread. "I didn't think she did either."

Bobby continued to stare at Cat's lifeless body.

"You were really feelin' her?"

Bobby nodded in response.

"You wanna get outta here, go home with Pam? I'll get Freeze and Nick to take care of this."

Bobby took the bedspread from Mike and laid it out on the floor next to her body. "No, Mike. This is my mess. I have to be the one to clean it up."

"You sure?" Mike and Bobby both knelt down and placed the body in the bedspread.

"Yeah, I'm sure. I'll be all right. Besides, the last thing I wanna do is go home with Pam. Let her and Shy bond, spend some more time together."

"Maybe the two of you should go away for a while, spend some time together," Mike suggested as they wrapped up the body.

"Maybe." Bobby paused. "You ready?"

"Yeah," Mike said, and together they carried Cat out of her apartment.

a story by roy glenn

Once they got her downstairs and in the trunk, Bobby started to take Pam home, but she insisted on going to her sister's house to pick up the children. Shy was able to convince her that she shouldn't be around her children in her current state of mind. Once Pam finally agreed to that, then she didn't want to go home.

"I keep thinking about you and her in our bed," Pam said.

Bobby remained quiet.

"Take her to my house then," Mike suggested and Pam agreed. Mike asked Shy if she would mind staying with her until they took care of things. Naturally, Shy agreed and said that they'd be fine. Bobby drove to Mike's house and took Pam inside. He stood by and watched in silence as Shy and Mike took her upstairs to his room and put her to bed. When they came back downstairs, Bobby went up and tried to talk to Pam.

"Bobby," Pam said without opening her eyes. "I think you should go help Mike. I know we need to talk, but this is not the time."

Bobby told Pam that he understood and gladly left her alone.

After Mike and Bobby left, Shy went upstairs to check on Pam. She told Shy that she was fine, and that she just wanted to get some rest. As Shy was about to go back downstairs, Pam said, "Shy."

"Yes, Pam."

"Where's my gun? I need my gun back."

"Michael has it. I'm sure he'll take care of it," Shy promised. "What do you need a gun for?"

"In case she comes back. She may try to get in the house again."

259

PAYBACK

"I don't think that's possible," Shy said and let out a little laugh. "Michael and Bobby are taking care of that right now."

"Do you have a gun?" Pam asked.

"No, Pam, I don't have a gun."

"Okay," Pam said and rolled over.

When Mike and Bobby drove off, they drove right past Melinda, who had been following them all night. After she left Freeze at Cuisine, Melinda went to Impressions to establish her alibi. She would stay there until the club closed, then go home to find D-Train's body. Once she found it, she planned to scream at the top of her lungs until one of her nosy-ass neighbors came to see what she was screaming about.

When Melinda got to the club, who were the first people she saw on the dance floor? Black and that bitch, Shy. It made her think about her great plan. *You mean Diego's great plan.*

Diego had realized the first time he met Melinda that she controlled D-Train. When Diego came to her and asked for her help in destroying everything that Black worked so hard to build, she gladly accepted. Black was never coming back to her, so why not?

It all was gonna be so easy, Melinda thought. She was going to get back at Black for dumping her. She would take apart the organization that she thought she knew so much about, piece by piece. Melinda would do it slowly, methodically, the way Black would do it.

And it would have worked if D-Train's people hadn't fucked everything up.

a story by roy glenn

But her plan changed the day that Sal Terrico dropped that bitch Shy in her lap. Melinda begged Diego to kill her, but he had other plans for the bitch. It was only after Melinda promised Diego that she wouldn't kill her, and that she would give him a little something else—*at least he was quick about it*—that Diego told Sal to deliver the bitch to D-Train. Then she came up with a new plan. She would convince D-Train to kill Shy. Once the bitch was dead, Melinda would tell Black. Black would kill D-Train and take him off her neck, which would leave her free to be there for Black in his time of need.

When D-Train slapped the shit outta her, Melinda knew that she had lost control of him, but the plan was still a good one. That night after she left The Spot, Melinda drove to 151st to the place where they were holding Shy. She would kill Shy herself and still tell Black that D-Train did it. But nobody was there when she got there.

It made her mad as hell to see them together, out on the dance floor that she and Black used to call their own. She hated that bitch, Shy, with a passion. Melinda decided that whether she got Black back or not, that bitch didn't deserve to live, even if it meant killing Black too.

When she saw them leaving the club with Bobby, Melinda followed them. She knew that there was a warrant out for that bitch Shy's arrest. It would be easier to simply call the police and tell them where she was. But that wasn't good enough.

With Black's power and Wanda thinking she's so fuckin' smart-ass, that bitch, Shy, would be out in no time.

PAYBACK

No, killing her was the only way Melinda could come home.

Melinda almost lost them when Bobby made that U-turn, but she was able to keep up. When she saw Shy leading Pam out of the building, she knew something was up. When she followed them around to the alley and saw Black and Bobby put what she was sure was a body in the trunk, she not only knew she had something, but she knew where Black and Bobby were going next. The parlor.

Mike and Bobby realized very early in their line of work that dead men do tell tales when you leave the bodies lying around for the cops to find. With that thought in mind, Mike bought a funeral parlor with a cremation furnace. It was a very efficient way to dispose of their enemies without a trace. The entire process usually took about two hours. Melinda knew she had plenty of time.

With Pam resting comfortably, Shy went back downstairs. Even though it was late, she wasn't tired, or maybe she was just too hyped over the events of the evening to sleep. So, she stretched out on the couch and turned on the television. While Shy channel surfed, her mind drifted to thoughts of Pam. There was still a part of her that couldn't believe that Pam had killed that woman.

But why not? You killed somebody when they pushed you to your limit. Pam did the same thing. Imagine how many women wish they could kill their man's other woman. The line would be long.

As she flipped from channel to channel and tried to get comfortable, Shy thought about all the times she'd accused Mike of flirting too much or having what she considered an inappropriate friendship with another woman. She'd even flat-out accused him of cheating, but it had never come to anything like this. No woman had ever called her or broke into their house.

"You might as well turn that off, 'cause there ain't ever anything on at this hour." A voice came from the shadows.

"Pam, is that you?"

"Don't you wish it was Pam?"

"Who's there?"

Melinda stepped into the light, and her gun was pointed at Shy.

"You." Shy thought she recognized the voice. It was the woman who wanted to kill her while she was being held captive. Shy stood up. "How did you get in here?"

"I used to live here until you came along, bitch," Melinda said and took another step closer to Shy.

"What do you want?"

"I'm here to take back what you took from me."

"What are you talkin' about?"

"I'm talkin' about Black, you stupid bitch."

"And you think—"

"Shut up, bitch," Melinda said calmly. "You ruined everything. I was happy. We were happy, happy with each other, bitch. Do you understand what that means? Do you understand how I felt?"

Shy remained quiet.

"No, I didn't think so. You couldn't possibly understand what this feels like."

"Yes, I can."

"Then you shouldn't have been fuckin' with my man. My man! Not yours, mine!" Melinda took a step closer and Shy backed into a corner. "Look at you.

PAYBACK

What does he see in you? What do you have that I don't? What the fuck is so special about you?"

Shy wanted to say, "Whatever it was, it was enough to take Michael away from you with ease, so you oughta check yourself." But not wanting her smart mouth to get her killed, she looked around the room for a weapon or a way out.

Melinda looked at the clock on the wall and knew she had to get this over with and get back to the club to establish her alibi. "Here's what's gonna happen now, bitch. I'm gonna kill you and that bitch upstairs. Black and Bobby are gonna think that D-Train's boys killed y'all in retaliation for Freeze killin' D-Train, and they'll wipe them off the face of the earth. Once that's over and Black starts to grieve over the loss of your bitch ass, I'll be there to help him put it back together."

"You don't have to do this," Shy pleaded with Melinda.

"Oh, yes I do. You don't deserve to have him. You don't deserve to have my man."

"We can talk about this, can't we?"

"Talk? Talk about what? How you snuck behind my back and stole my man? Is that what we should talk about, bitch? I don't think so. What do you think? That if you keep me here talking, Black will come and save your worthless bitch ass? Well, you can forget about that. I saw the body him and Bobby carried out. What your girl Pam do, kill somebody?"

Shy didn't answer.

"It doesn't matter. You don't have to answer me, bitch. I know they took that body to the parlor, and if they did, it'll be at least two hours before they get finished, so nobody is coming to save you."

If that was the case, Shy figured, since she was going to die, she might as well speak her mind and die with dignity.

"You know what?" Shy started. "Damn, I don't even remember what your name is. Never was all that important. But I guess it doesn't matter now. I guess nothing matters now, so let me tell you something. Mike Black is my man, *bitch.* Not your man, my man." Shy held up her left hand. "This big-ass fuckin' rock on my finger proves that he's my man. He may have been your man, but you weren't woman enough to hold him, and that's why he's my man. And by the way, you never lived here. You may have got fucked here, but live here, in my house? No, I don't think so. So, go ahead and kill me, you dumb bitch, 'cause even if you kill me, Mike Black will always be my man."

Melinda grabbed the gun with both hands and cocked the hammer. Shy heard the shot, closed her eyes, and prepared to die.

But nothing happened.

Shy opened her eyes in time to see Melinda drop the gun and fall to the floor.

Pam stepped out of the shadows with a gun in her hand. She stood over Melinda's body. "These bitches got to learn to stop fuckin' with somebody else's man."

Shy smiled. "Where'd you get the gun?" she asked as she kicked the gun away from Melinda.

"I know where Mike keeps his guns."

"Well, wherever you got it, Pam, thank you. You saved my life." Shy walked over to the phone and dialed Bobby's cell phone number. "Hi, Bobby, it's Shy. I know y'all are busy, but it's important. Can I speak to Michael?"

PAYBACK

Bobby handed his phone to Mike. "Hello, baby, what's up?"

"Like I told Bobby, I know y'all are busy, but when you get finished with that one, Pam's got another one ready for the parlor."

After Shy called, Mike left Bobby to run the cremation furnace while he went to see what Shy was talking about. When he got to his house, Mike was more than surprised to see a woman's body lying on his living room floor. He was even more shocked to see that it was Melinda.

Mike turned as Shy walked up behind him.

"Friend of yours?" Shy mused. She wrapped her arms around his waist.

"What was she doin' here?"

"I didn't invite her. All of a sudden she was just there." Shy handed him a blanket.

"What happened, baby?"

"She came to get *her man* back."

Chapter Forty-five

Eight o'clock was fast approaching, and it found Diego Estabon sitting by the phone, waiting for his father's kidnappers to call. He took a moment to consider the fact that earlier today he had five million dollars deposited in his account, and now he was waiting to pay five million for the safe return of his father. *Just another one of life's little ironies.* It wasn't about the money. He could and most likely would get the money back from Gomez.

He'll probably insist on giving me back my money. He wouldn't want me to have that type of power over him.

Finally, the phone rang and Diego quickly answered. "This is Diego."

"Bring the money to the pier at Sag Harbor. Come alone or your father dies violently," the same digitally disguised voice said and quickly disconnected the call.

Diego put out his cigar, finished his drink and thought one last time about not paying the ransom. Since he knew he had left himself no choice to the matter, Diego picked up the briefcase with the money and drove out to Sag Harbor. Before he left, Diego instructed his men to give him a ten-minute head start and then head out to the harbor, just in case.

When Diego arrived at the pier, he got out of his car and walked up and down the pier with five million dollars, but his phone never rang. He never was a patient man, and he hated being kept waiting. All he wanted to do was get this over with.

Then a very pretty Latino woman dressed in a very short skirt and a very tight T-shirt began walking toward him. Diego's smile widened as she got closer.

"Hello, Diego," the woman said and stopped in front of him. Before he could speak to her, Diego felt the gun in his back.

"Hello, Diego," the gunman said while relieving Diego of his weapon and handing it to the woman.

"You will come with me," the woman said and led Diego to a small boat. Diego's men got there in time to see them leave the dock. While the man watched Diego, the woman piloted the boat out to sea. As they got closer to it, Diego knew that he was being taken to his father's boat.

"You are holding my father hostage on board his own boat?"

The man and woman looked at each other and laughed. Once they reached the boat, Diego was taken aboard and brought to the upper deck. When they got there, one man stood on deck waiting.

"Mike Black."

"Hello, Diego, my friend," Mike said.

"I should have known it was you, but I didn't think you were this stupid. Of course you know that I am going to kill you for this."

"That remains to be seen."

"Kill you the way I should have a long time ago."

Quickly becoming bored with Diego's threats, Black said, "Whatever, Diego, just put the money on that table and back away from it."

"Where is Gomez? I want to see that my father is safe first."

"Diego, you are in absolutely no position to even think about callin' any shots."

"Where is Gomez?" Diego shouted.

"Calm down and stop shouting, Diego. I'm right here."

Diego turned quickly and saw his father coming out of the cabin with a drink in one hand and a woman on his arm.

"Papa?" a very confused Diego said as Gomez stood next to Mike.

"He was always very excitable as a boy," Gomez said to Mike. "Don't look so confused, Diego."

"What is going on, Papa?"

"It should be obvious, even to you, what is going on, Diego," Gomez said and turned to Mike. "He was a slow learner as well. I would always have to explain things two or three times before he would understand me."

"Why are you telling him these things, Papa?"

"A whiner, too," Gomez whispered.

"Stop it!" Diego shouted. "Why do you always find a way to embarrass me?"

"See? What did I tell you? Very excitable. You must learn to calm down and relax."

"I am calm, Papa. Just tell me what is going on."

PAYBACK

"I was never kidnapped, Diego," Gomez said and put his arm around his son. "I was never a hostage on board my own yacht. That would be embarrassing. Black came to see me. He came with respect, Diego, something else you must learn."

"I must learn?" Diego jerked away from Gomez.

"When Black told me about the things you've done, I was ashamed to be called your father."

"So you went along with this kidnapping idea?"

"No, Diego. The kidnapping was my idea," Gomez told him. "Why do you treat this man with disrespect? We have no quarrel with this man. His business is not our business, and he has not interfered with our business. You must make me understand why you chose to do this, Diego."

"Papa, you are taking his side over mine again."

"Not his side, Diego, the right side. The honorable side. I blame myself for this. It was I who allowed his mother to spoil him as a boy. She breastfed him well past his second birthday." Everybody on deck laughed at Diego, who by this time was fed up.

"Shut up! Shut up, I said!"

"Diego," Gomez said calmly. "Did you bring the money?"

"The money!" Diego yelled.

"Yes, Diego, the ransom money. Did you bring it?"

"Yes, I have it."

"Give it to me," Gomez said

"You put me through this for nothing! Then you bring me out here and embarrass me in front of this dead man—and I am going to kill you, Black."

"Whatever, Diego," Mike said and smiled at him.

"Now you want the money. Well, here is my answer!" Diego reached in the briefcase and pulled out a gun. He began walking toward Mike and Gomez, shooting wildly. Mike grabbed Gomez and they hit the deck. The man and woman both fired at Diego. The man hit Diego in the back, but he didn't go down. When the woman hit him in the arm, he dropped his gun. The man grabbed Diego around the neck. "I'll kill you!" he yelled and struggled to get free. The man hit Diego in the back of the head with his gun, and Diego slumped to the ground.

Mike helped Gomez get up from the deck. "Take Diego below," Gomez said. "Have my doctor give him something to make him sleep for a while."

Gomez turned to Mike. "What have I done, Black? I never meant for it to come to this."

"I'm sorry, Gomez," Mike said and put his hand on his gun just in case.

"Don't be. It was not your fault. I never thought that Diego would try to kill me. You should go now, Black. My people will take you back to shore."

"What about Diego?" Mike asked.

"I'll take him back to Peru. You have nothing to fear from Diego."

Mike bowed slightly in a gesture of respect to Gomez and turned to walk away.

"Aren't you forgetting something?" Gomez asked.

"What's that?" Mike said and turned slowly with his hand still on his gun. He expected to see Gomez standing with a gun pointed at him, but was surprised to see him holding out Diego's briefcase.

"The money. Take it."

"I can't do that, Gomez. It wouldn't be right. Diego took no money from me. I can't take his money," Mike lied, knowing that he had already taken some of Diego's money.

"I insist, Black," Gomez said.

"Of course, Gomez," Mike said and took the briefcase.

Gomez's people took Mike ashore where Bobby was waiting. On the way, Mike thought about how things had turned out. Earlier that day, he had Jackie and Vonda pay a visit to Frontier Pharmaceuticals, dressed in short dresses and showing plenty of cleavage. Most of the men and quite a few of the women in the building were too distracted to notice Jackie when she attached a keystroke emulator to the computer in the main conference room, where, hours later, Diego would complete his transaction. At that point, it was easy for Travis, with Monika's help, to hack into their network and get the password to Diego's account. Once the money was transferred in, Travis transferred it out to another account. Mike got off the boat and walked toward Bobby's car, thinking that there was one other person he needed to see.

Chapter Forty-six

Mike was tired when Bobby dropped him off at his house. He got in bed with Shy, but he didn't sleep long. A few hours later, Mike was up and reaching for the phone. He paused a moment and looked at Shy. Maybe he shouldn't do this. Maybe he should wake Shy, get her dressed, head straight for the airport, and take her back to their quiet life on the island. Mike knew if he didn't take care of this now, then it would only come up over and over, and he would have to deal with it sooner or later.

He started to get up and leave the room so Shy could sleep, but since it was about her anyway, she might as well wake up. Mike ran his fingers through Shy's hair. "Baby," Mike said and touched her face. "Wake up."

"Morning, baby. Is everything all right?"

"I gotta make a call." Mike dialed a number.

"Okay, and you woke me up because?"

"You'll see," Mike said as the phone rang.

"This is Kirk."

"Good morning, Kirk. This is Mike Black."

PAYBACK

"Morning, Black. I knew sooner or later you'd be calling."

"I'd like to talk to you, detective. Is there someplace I could meet you?"

"Castle Hill Diner, say in an hour? You can buy me lunch," Kirk said.

"See you there."

A little over an hour later, Mike and Shy walked hand in hand into the Castle Hill Diner. Kirk was already there. He rose to his feet when he saw them coming toward him.

"How's it goin', Kirk?" Mike said and extended his hand.

"Doin' good," Kirk replied and shook Mike's hand.

"Kirk, this is my wife, Cassandra."

Shy held out her hand. "Please call me Shy."

"Mrs. Black, it is a pleasure to finally meet you. I was told that you were the most beautiful woman on the face of the earth. I see now that I was not deceived," Kirk said graciously. "Please, have a seat."

Once they were seated, the waitress brought out Kirk's food. "I hope you don't mind, I went ahead and ordered."

"Not at all, detective," Mike said. "Go ahead and enjoy your meal."

"So, Black, what did you want to see me about?"

"I wanted to talk to you about the DEA investigating me for drug trafficking. Kirk, you know I don't do that kind of business."

"I know. She does, or at least she used to."

Shy fought off the urge to defend herself, and remained quiet. She would have her chance later.

"You don't you to worry about the DEA, at least for now, Black."

Mike glanced at Shy. "Why is that, detective?"

"The operation's been terminated," Kirk said as he ate. "After I talked to Simmons and his story didn't jive with the official version the DEA was puttin' out, I did some checkin' on my own."

"What was the official version?" Mike asked.

"That the lovely Mrs. Black here was involved in a meeting with know drug dealers."

"I was?" Shy said, no longer able to hold her tongue. "Was that before or after they kidnapped me?"

Mike touched her hand. "Go on, detective."

"We checked with the Bahamian police and they confirmed Simmons' story."

"We? Who is we?"

"The New York City police department."

"Why is the NYPD helping me?"

Kirk put down his fork. "Understand this, Black. We weren't helping you. The DEA came to us to help them get you. Their shit was incorrect. Excuse my French, Mrs. Black. Black, you're a lot of things: you're a gambler, you're a pimp, you're a thief, and a killer. But the one thing that you aren't is a drug dealer. Everybody knows that, so we started looking at agent DeFrancisco and his finances. Nice house in Annapolis, Maryland. More house than he could afford in his salary. He also had a beach front house in Nags Head, North Carolina and a boat. Thirty-footer."

"Sounds like somebody's on the take."

"You think?"

Mike and Shy laughed.

PAYBACK

"We took what we found to the DEA and they found that the intelligence DeFrancisco used to get authorization for the operation was fake. Now we're trying to find out what Martin Marshall's got to do with any of this."

"What makes you think he's involved?" Mike asked, not yet ready to share what he knew.

"When DeFrancisco came to us for help, Marshall came with him."

"It's funny that you should mention Senator Marshall," Mike said, knowing his information would be worth something to Kirk.

"Why's that, Black?"

"How would you like to not only link Marshall to DeFrancisco, but tag him for murder?"

"I'm listening."

Shy reached in her purse and put a CD on the table in front of Kirk.

"What's that?"

"It's a recording of the senator discussing with the killer his involvement in a murder of a woman," Shy told him. "And a recording of a conversation between Senator Marshall and Diego Estabon. It might interest you to know that they were discussing Agent DeFrancisco."

"Where did you get that?" Kirk asked.

"Does it matter?"

"No, it doesn't, 'cause nothing on that disk would be admissible in court."

"But you would know all the right questions to ask 'cause you already know the answers," Shy said. "You interested?"

"I'm interested." Kirk reached for the disk.

Shy put her hand on it. "In exchange for . . ." She paused. "In exchange for your assistance in getting those false charges against me dropped."

Kirk took his hand off the disk and ate another piece of his steak. The detective sat back in the booth and put down his knife and fork. He looked at Shy and thought about her offer and then to Black, who had remained silent. Kirk reached in his pocket and took out his cell phone. He dialed a number.

"Detective Sanchez."

"Gene, this is Kirk. Listen, you speak to the ADA about dropping the charges against Cassandra Sims yet?"

"Not yet, Kirk, why?"

"Go ahead and call her. We got bigger fish to fry."

"Done," Sanchez said. "Who's the fish?"

"I'll tell you when I see you," Kirk promised and hung up his phone.

"Just like that?" Shy asked, letting go of the disk. "One word from you and the charges are dropped?"

"Did I mention what a good job your lawyer, Wanda Moore, was doing?" Kirk got up and threw a couple of dollars on the table for a tip. "Yeah, just the other day Detective Sanchez said that he was going to have to drop the charges against you. He was gettin' a lot of pressure from the ADA, who was gettin' pressure from your lawyer. He was gonna drop the charges against you anyway." Kirk held up the disk. "But thanks for this. I never liked Marshall anyway."

Mike and Shy watched Kirk walk out. "I'm free, baby," she said and kissed him. "Now I can stay in New York."

PAYBACK

"We can go anywhere you want," Mike said and got up from the table. "Just one more thing left to do," he said and paid the check.

Epilogue

One year later on an island off the west coast of Mexico . . .

Diego Estabon sat alone in his bungalow, waiting for his new partners to arrive with his share of their last job. They were late, very late.

It had been a good year for Diego, and he planned for next year to be even better. The phone rang. "It's about time you called. Where are you?"

"I'm right outside, Diego," Mike said into the phone.

Diego rushed to the window and saw Mike standing off in the distance.

"What do you want, Black?" Diego said and quickly armed himself.

"As soon as Sal told you that he had kidnapped my wife, you should have told Sal to let her out the car and apologize for taking her," Mike said and hung up the phone.

Diego watched as Mike turned to walk away. He wondered what that was all about. Then he thought it would probably be a good idea if got outta there. But

279

PAYBACK

before Diego could make it to the door, the bungalow blew up.

As he walked away, Mike felt the heat of the explosion on the back of his neck. *Now it's over.*